The Little Tree That Changed Everything

December 7, 2019

To ELOISE,

I Hope You ENJOY MY
VERY FIRST BOOK! I WILL
HAVE ANOTHER BOOK ABOUT A
FAIRY PRINCESS NEXT YEAR!
THANKS!

David R. Gaslin

PAGE PUBLISHING, INC.
Conneaut Lake, PA

First originally published by Page Publishing 2019

ISBN 978-1-64584-133-3 (pbk)
ISBN 978-1-64584-134-0 (digital)

Printed in the United States of America

To the love of my life, Ruthie; our precious children, Amanda, Adam, Dennis, and Carrie; and our priceless grandchildren, Alexandria, Genevieve, Sebastian, and Adelyn.

Each of you lights my way and makes me try harder to be the very best I can be.

The Way Things Began

When Ruthie woke up, it was still dark outside. All she could hear were two very distinct sounds—the wind swirling around her home and the soft, snuffling snores of her goldendoodle, Daisy, lying asleep on the rug by her bed. She eased out of bed as quietly as possible so as not to disturb the dog, who would immediately want to go and explore outside. She slid into her slippers, padded softly to the window, and pulled the curtain aside.

Outside, all you could see was the star at the top of the giant Christmas tree at the far end of the property. She could see snowflakes—big, puffy ones—hitting the window and quickly melting away from the warmth of her house. The forecast was clear and cold for the day. The way the snow was falling, it shouldn't accumulate much. The long curving driveway that led down to the main road shouldn't need to be cleared. This was especially good since all four of her grandchildren—Alexandria, Genevieve, Sebastian, and Adelyn—were home from college and coming to spend the night. It was going to be a great afternoon and evening!

She had much to do, so she put on her flannel robe (over her flannel pajamas, of course) and made her way quietly out of the bedroom and into the kitchen. She put on a pot of coffee and turned on her old radio. She tuned it to the station that played continuous Christmas music at this time of year. She went to the fireplace where Toby, the farm foreman, had piled wood and kindling the afternoon before so she could easily get the fire going. It was a big fireplace that opened into the kitchen, by the kitchen table, and it also opened into the large great room with all the big comfy chairs. She thought of all the great times and stories that had been shared in both rooms and throughout this wonderful old house. She smiled at the thought and lit the kindling.

Ruthie went back to the coffee maker, poured herself a hot cup of coffee, and sat down at the table. There was one slice left of the vanilla cream pound cake that she had made. She had cut the cake in quarters when she first baked it, giving one quarter each to Toby, Consuela (the cleaning lady), and Hiram, who tended the yard. Of the quarter cake she had kept, there was only one slice left. The last slice would make a wonderful breakfast along with the coffee!

She began to make a list of what she would need from the pantry. Alexandria, Genevieve, and Adelyn all wanted to come over to bake and decorate Christmas cookies. Each one had a different favorite of their grandmother's cookie recipes. There would be lots of fun, joy, and laughter today! Sebastian wasn't into baking or decorating the cookies, but he had said he guessed he "had to come in order to sample the cookies and make sure they were edible." He had also insisted that for the dinner tonight, they have Grandma's homemade chili and cornbread. The girls all quickly agreed as they loved Grandma's cooking, but especially her chili and cornbread!

Ruthie put out the various cookie recipes on the long kitchen counter and the necessary ingredients close by. It was starting to get light outside when Daisy shuffled into the kitchen, nuzzled up against Ruthie's leg, and waited for her head and back to be patted. The wait wasn't long, and Ruthie let Daisy outside to go and do her business. The dog ran to her favorite spot in the yard, squatted for less than a minute, and immediately returned. Ruthie laughed as this dog with the long curly blond fur immediately ran over and laid down in front of the fireplace where the fire was burning brightly.

The grands were all coming over after lunch, so Ruthie began to make the cornbread first. It was an old family recipe that had many ingredients, but the favorite ingredients were the jalapeno slices and cheddar cheese. She finished up the cornbread and put it aside so the flavors could mingle. She would bake it fresh, right before dinner, and serve it hot out the oven. Now she got her big old chili pot out. She began dicing the tomatoes, then the onions. She browned the meat and added her special seasonings into the mixture. Lastly, she added the kidney beans, both light and dark. She put it on the stove and set it to simmer for a few hours. She cleaned the utensils and bowls she had used, dried them, and put them all back in their rightful places.

It was almost lunchtime now, so she made herself a quick sandwich, washed it down with sweet iced tea, and went to her bedroom to change clothes. She took a hot shower, brushed her teeth, ran a brush over and through her silver hair, put on a little makeup, and dressed for the afternoon, There was no need—well, maybe a little—to worry about getting ingredients on their clothes. She had ordered five special aprons, each with their name and job embroidered on the front. There was Grandma ("head baker" printed underneath), and Alexandria, Genevieve, and Adelyn all had "cookie baker" embroidered underneath. Sebastian's read "cookie taster." Daisy even had a small cape which read "if anything hits the floor, it's mine."

It was almost 1:00 p.m. when she heard the car honking from a distance. She hurried to the front window to look outside. She could see Alexandria's car turning off the main road, and right behind her was Sebastian in his car. As they came closer, honking all the way up the driveway, she could see Alexandria laughing at something her sister, Genevieve, had said. Genevieve was waving her hands around and laughing like it was the funniest thing ever. As they pulled to a stop in the driveway, Sebastian and his sister, Adelyn, pulled in beside them. They were laughing as they got out of their car, singing "Jingle Bells."

Alexandria got out, scooped up a handful of snow, and tossed it at Sebastian. Her throw went wide, but Genevieve's aim was on the mark, lightly bouncing off Sebastian's shoulder. Sebastian turned around with a shocked look, and Genevieve laughed out loud. Sebastian said, "I'll get you, G," and gathered up his own handful of snow. She watched them throwing handfuls of the soft powdery snow at each other, dodging behind their cars and laughing. It was so obvious how very much they loved each other. After a few minutes, she opened the front door. They heard the door open and saw Ruthie standing there, trying to conceal her smile. Daisy ran excitedly out to join the fun, jumping and barking. They all happily greeted Daisy, laughed, and ran into Grandma's outstretched arms.

They wiped their feet on the mat and shook the snow off their coats. Sebastian held the door open for all of them as they went inside. Alexandria had her arm in her grandmother's as they all went into the great room and collapsed onto the furniture. Genevieve was excitedly telling Adelyn about the swimming competitions she had been in and how she had done. Adelyn was just as excited and kept interrupting to talk about her latest boyfriend and how special he was. Sebastian was looking around the room, taking it all in and remembering all the fun they had all enjoyed there. The sleepovers, the parties, every Christmas day, it had always been magical. Alexandria was telling Ruthie about her studies, her grades, and how much she was enjoying her time at the University of Florida. They spent an hour or more just catching up. At last, Ruthie said, "Well, if we are going to bake cookies, I guess we'd better get to it." They all headed into the kitchen.

Alexandria spent the afternoon making her favorite candy cane cookies. After making a large batch of cookie dough, she divided this in half and then added red food coloring to one batch. She then made pencil-sized pieces out of the two batches, carefully twirling one from each batch together to form the candy cane. Lastly, she curled the top over, placed it on the cookie sheet, and sprinkled it with crushed peppermint candies. Adelyn was making large snowflake cookies. After these were baked, she delicately decorated each one with pale blue icing and tiny silver candy balls. Lastly, G was in charge of the cutout cookies; if there was a cookie cutter, she used it. She had four tubes of frosting from the store and six more frosting colors she had concocted. There were also tiny multicolored candies she liberally sprinkled on. Her area, though controlled, looked like a peacock had exploded. Her cookies though were truly works of art. Sebastian sat back and relished his job. Not counting his mother and auntie, he was being fed warm fresh Christmas cookies by the four women he loved more than anything else. He was also able to sneak Daisy an occasional cookie.

At last, all the ingredients had been used, the cookies had all been baked, and the kitchen had been cleaned up. Sebastian went out to the woodpile to gather up more logs to get the fire blazing brightly again while the girls finished putting all the cookies in assorted Tupperware containers.

When Sebastian returned, he said, "I can't believe I'm saying this, but I'm getting kind of hungry. I think it's the smell of Grandma's chili!"

Everyone laughed, chiming in, "Me too, me too, me too."

Ruthie said, "Let me bake the cornbread, and we will eat in about twenty minutes, okay?"

They all nodded enthusiastically, taking their aprons off and placing them in the laundry room.

After a little bit, Ruthie had a large basket of cornbread ready. She ladled a bowl full of chili for each precious young adult. Each one took their spoon and bowl and went into the dining room. When they got to the table, they all just stopped and looked around, almost in a state of reverence.

Ruthie entered and asked, "What's wrong?"

Alexandria turned to her with a tear on her cheek and said, "I think we are all just remembering how talented Granddaddy was and how much he loved all of us." As talented a woodworker, furniture maker, and carver as their great grandpa had been, he had been no match for their granddaddy.

The dining room table had been made from four large planks that had been sanded down and varnished. The two twin pedestals that supported the table were each carved and beautiful. These, however, were no match for the chairs. Each chair had one of the grandchildren's names carved into it. All around the name and down the spokes that supported the top, Granddaddy had carved what they loved most. Sebastian had footballs, basketballs, and baseball players in action, throwing and catching. Adelyn's chair was intricately carved with all different kinds of designs, almost like a fairy spider web. G's chair was covered with carvings of purses, dresses, sunglasses, and high heels. It was the perfect chair for the fashion diva. Alexandria's chair was covered with her beloved horses. Some were running, some were grazing, and some were walking. They were all spectacular.

Grandma's and Granddaddy's chairs were different. Grandma's chair had her name carved into it. Around her name, Granddaddy had carved each grandchild's face and filled in the space with hearts. Granddaddy's chair said "Granddaddy." Around his name he had carved the faces of their grandchildren's parents, his and Ruthie's children: Amanda, Adam, Dennis, and Carrie. The chairs had all been a surprise. He had kept them in the barn and didn't reveal them to anyone until they were all finished. He and Ruthie ate many meals at that table. He always joked that he wanted to eat "with the whole family."

On top of the sideboard was the carving he was most famous for. It was an angel with the wings spread upward and outward behind. You could see every single feather in sharp detail. The angel's face was beautiful and looking upward. The expression on her face was one of adoration. Her arms came together in front, and her hands were folded in prayer. The folds in her gown were perfect as they fell to the ground, leaving only the tops of her bare feet showing. The back side of the angel was just as perfect. This angel had started out as just a picture out of a Facebook story about Henry and Ruthie. The photo had gone viral.

Many had tracked Henry down, offering him unbelievable sums for this angel. Henry always had politely refused. He had told them he needed to keep her close to him to always remember how he owed everything to God. He wanted to remember to always be thankful and pray. Lastly, he always wanted to be reminded to pray for forgiveness, not only for himself but for everyone.

They all sat down in their chairs and enjoyed the dinner. As a special treat, Ruthie had made her famous peach cobbler. The kids had all said they were "too full for dessert" until she told them what it was. Sebastian, who was by now contentedly burping Christmas cookie aromas, asked if there was vanilla ice cream to go with it. Ruthie said, "Of course." After dessert, they all helped to clean up. Pretty quickly, the kitchen and dining room were spotless. They all trudged into the great room again. Sebastian stoked the fire to get it blazing again. Grandma sat down in her favorite chair, putting her feet up and covering herself with a warm knitted wool afghan. Daisy came over, circling her bed twice, and then collapsing contentedly into it.

It suddenly got very quiet. All you could hear were the soft Christmas carols still playing on the radio. Sebastian looked at Alexandria, who gave him an almost imperceptible nod. He turned to his grandmother and said, "Grandma, we were all talking this morning on the phone before coming over. Could you please tell all of us the story?"

Grandma smiled, and even though she knew better, she asked, "What story? The 'Night before Christmas'?"

They all laughed, and Sebastian said, "No, Grandma. Tell us the story of the ugly little Christmas tree. No one tells it like you do."

Grandma smiled and said, "I would love to share it with all of you again."

*****

A long time ago, your granddaddy, Henry, woke up in the bedroom you will be sleeping in tonight, Sebastian. Sebastian smiled. Henry heard the wind blowing outside. The forecast was for partly cloudy skies and snow. Henry really loved the snow. Today was going to be a very special day. His father had promised him that today they would go to the Christmas tree farm. Not only would they pick out their tree for the great room, but also Henry could pick out a small one to dig up and bring back to plant in their yard. Henry loved Christmas music, the Christmas season, all things Christmas, but *especially* Christmas trees! He could think of nothing better than having his own tree to take care of, to nurture and help it to grow straight and tall—a tree to decorate every year.

Henry eased out of bed and reached for his crutch. Henry had been born with a crooked leg. Due to the high cost of surgery and the lack of income, the family could not afford to have his leg fixed. Henry had grown up used to the crooked leg. Now that he was almost eight, he got around fairly quickly using the very special crutch his father had carved just for him. Since he had been old enough to look out the windows, he had always been fascinated by all the small animals scampering around outside. There were squirrels and chipmunks, skunks and rabbits, possums and birds of many colors. He had even once seen a few deer with their majestic antlers. Just as these animals were outside, his father had lovingly carved them into Henry's first crutch. These animals scampered into and around his crutch, all the way up to where one deer's head, with the antlers back behind him, formed the armrest. The crutch, with all its artwork, was almost four feet tall, and Henry treasured it!

He made his way to the closet and picked out his warm clothes: heavy wool socks, jeans, long-sleeved flannel shirt, sweater, and his goose down jacket (just like his daddy's). He quickly got dressed and made his way out to the kitchen where Mom and Dad were sitting at the kitchen table.

Henry's father looked around with an amused smile and asked, "Henry, do you have any plans for today?" They all laughed at that as Henry was already at the back door.

Henry's mother asked, "What about breakfast?"

Henry said, "Oh, I almost forgot" as he headed to the refrigerator. "I made myself a peanut butter and jelly sandwich and put milk in my thermos last night. I didn't want to delay us leaving today. I can have my breakfast on the road!" He grabbed his bag and thermos and headed back to the door. "Come on, Daddy! Let's go!" Henry's father got up, put his coat on, kissed Henry's mother, and headed out the door.

They went out to the barn and opened the doors. There she was. Not one of the big powerful trucks like today, but instead a truck so old it was almost an antique. It had big running boards and a tailgate that sometimes didn't work, but an engine that started up every time made the truck a keepsake. The truck's original color of red was still visible but had dimmed somewhat with age. Because of her color, Henry had named the truck Rosie. The comfy cab only sat three, but that was all they needed. Henry's father used the truck to deliver the furniture and various carvings he made for his customers.

As they pulled out onto the main road, Henry's father asked, "Since we have space for three, do you want to stop by Bruce's house and see if he would like to ride with us?" Henry had met Bruce in kindergarten almost three years ago, and they had been immediate friends. They each often referred to each other as lifelong friends.

Henry said, "That is a great idea!"

After stopping by to pick up Bruce, they made their way out to the tree farm. When they pulled in, Henry's father pointed out the big cardboard boxes in the shed. The boxes all contained Christmas tree stands. The boys excitedly got out of the car with Henry's father following behind.

The threesome moved up and down several rows before Henry spotted the most perfect tree for the great room. It was a noble fir, about six feet tall. They all walked carefully around the tree, looking for blemishes or imperfections but could find none. Before they could cut down this tree and remove it, they needed to find the tree lot owner and agree on a price. Henry's father said he would do that, and the two friends could continue looking for Henry's small tree to dig up and take home to plant.

Each grouping of trees had hand-printed signs in front of them, designating what they were. There were Fraser Firs, noble firs, cedar trees, and so many more. The boys marched up and down the rows looking. All of a sudden, Henry's father heard Henry calling, "Dad! Dad! I've found it! My perfect tree! Hurry up! Come and see!" Henry's father began to trot over to where his son was, unprepared for what he was about to see.

As Henry's father came around a break in the trees, there was Henry, nearly jumping up and down. He was so excited. Bruce, however, had a surprised look on his face. Someone had used a black marker to write "The Tree That Nobody Wanted" on a large piece of cardboard. Next to the sign was the scrawniest, most crooked, almost needle bare tree Henry's father had ever seen. It only had four branches, the top was curled over, and one tiny pine cone hung from it.

Henry's father knelt down and said, "Henry, you don't want this tree. You want to have one that you can watch grow straight and tall over the years. This little tree seems almost dead. It has been in the shadow of all the big trees around it for too many years. The other trees absorbed all the sunlight while it sat in their shade. They got the fertilizer, and this one didn't. This tree is only going to disappoint you."

Henry put his hand out and touched his father's face. He said, "Daddy, what you don't see that I see is this tree's heart. All the years with those trees growing bigger and bigger around it, blocking out more and more sunlight, this little tree refused to give up. It continued to stretch upward, just like me! It didn't give in or give up! This year it even produced a little pinecone. It believes in life. It is a fierce little tree. It wants to live and grow. It only needs a little sunshine, fertilizer, and love. I can give it all three. *Please*, Daddy, let me take this tree home."

With tears in his eyes, his daddy agreed. They paid for the noble fir, cut it down, and laid it in the truck bed. The owner wouldn't even charge them for Henry's tree. They quickly dug it up, set it gently in the truck bed, and headed home.

When they returned home, after dropping the still surprised Bruce off at his house, Henry went to work. He wouldn't let anyone help him. First, he asked his mother and father if he could plant the little tree in the front yard. He wanted to keep a close eye on the tree, and he wanted, one day, for his friends down in the valley to be able to see it. They didn't think the little tree would survive the winter, but they couldn't disappoint Henry, so they agreed. Henry scraped the snow four feet away on all sides from where he wanted to plant the tree. With a little help from his daddy, he dug the large hole. He poured some potting soil in first and then fertilizer. He gently unwrapped the roots, which had grown tighter and tighter around each other because previously there was no room for them to grow outward. He placed the tree gently into the hole and filled in the hole with the dirt. He talked to the little tree the whole time, saying, "Welcome to your new home, little tree. There is no need to be scared anymore or be in the shadows. I am here. I will take care of you and love you every day. All you have to do is do what you were made to do. Just grow to be the tree you were meant to be. I love you, little tree."

When the weather turned colder, he and Daddy made a little shelter to put over the tree. Henry ran an electric cord into the little shelter and plugged a light bulb in to warm the tree and keep the roots from freezing. Each day, no matter how cold or windy it was, Henry went outside to the little shelter to wipe away any accumulated snow and check on the tree. Each day, he got down on his knees to talk to the little tree, saying, "Hang in there, little tree. Spring is coming. You are going to love spring. All the grass comes back and turns green. The birds all come back and sing in the trees. All the flowers bloom. It's a beautiful time. Hang in there." When the cold weather ended, they stored the shelter and light bulb, although Henry believed it would need to be much bigger next year.

Spring came, and as the new needles appeared on the tree, so did two pine cones! The tree also seemed to be getting straighter. Henry stopped by the tree at least twice daily—once before school to confide any test fears and at least once a day after school to tell the little tree all the good things that had happened. It was the little tree that first heard about the little girl in his third-grade class that was "the most beautiful girl in the world." He was madly in love with her. Her name was Ruthie.

The little tree continued to enjoy time with Henry. Now in the afternoons, sometimes Ruthie and Bruce would join him. They would sit cross-legged on the ground and talk about their days. No one but Henry ever talked to the tree, but he believed the tree enjoyed their company. For Henry's ninth birthday, his father carved a new crutch, this one an homage to all things *Star Wars* which Henry had become a fanatic about. Luke, Leia, Han Solo, Darth Vader, and even Yoda were represented among the planets on his crutch.

Every year, the tree grew a little straighter and taller. Each year it produced even more pine cones. Henry would carefully gather up the seeds and take them back to a secret place deep on the property that no one knew about. The family had owned almost five hundred acres for several generations. Each generation had pledged that no matter what, they would not divide up or sell off any of the land. There was plenty of vacant land in the huge parcel.

Grade school ended and became middle school. Henry liked all his teachers, and they all liked him very much. Henry really worked hard at his grades, and the results showed it. He did very well on all the tests too. He had many good friends but, by now, he, Bruce, and Ruthie were nearly inseparable.

In her tenth-grade year, Ruthie was required to write an article about someone that was her hero. She wrote about her very best friend Henry and titled her article "The Boy That Saw What Others Couldn't." She described how he came from a family of heroes. No matter what happened in their lives, they persevered. They never seemed hurt, angry, or sad. They were always first to help others in need. She wrote that at an early age, Henry had shown that same spirit when he rescued "his little Christmas tree that nobody wanted."

She went on in great detail, explaining the history of the tree and including pictures of its growth from frail little tree to the towering, nearly forty-foot tall tree it was today. The tree had filled out and was deep green, bushy, and full. She compared Henry and the tree. He had been a frail little boy with a crutch when she first became his friend. Now, although still using a crutch, he was healthy, strong, and almost six feet tall. She finished the story by showing examples of the wood carvings and furniture that Henry and his father created. They often donated pieces for auction to help any local families in need. When Ruthie asked Henry's father why they donated the pieces instead of selling them, he said his family had always been blessed with all they needed, and "although we cannot help others by giving them money, we can use our gifts in order to help those in need in other ways."

Ruthie's teacher was so impressed that not only did Ruthie get an A, but also, with her permission, he submitted it to an online digest of inspirational articles. It was quickly copied and spread throughout the Internet and throughout social media, having been viewed thousands and thousands of times.

One afternoon, after Henry returned from school, the family's landline rang. Henry's mother answered. And then, with a shocked look, turned to Henry and said, "It's for you."

Henry took the phone from his mother and said, "Hello?"

The very businesslike female voice asked, "Mr. Henry Taggart?"

Henry said, "Yes."

The lady on the other end said, "Please hold one moment for the president of the United States."

Henry immediately sat down on the big comfy sofa. A moment later, he heard the world-famous deep baritone voice of President John Forrester on the phone. "Henry? Are you there?"

Henry answered, "Yes, Mr. President. I am here."

President Forrester continued, "Henry, my staff and I have been reading all about you and your magnificent tree. We are all so thrilled with all your hard work and selfless giving, both for your tree and your community. Your country needs to hear your story. I am so proud of you and your family."

Henry could barely speak. He said, "Thank you, Mr. President."

President Forrester said, "I would really like the country to meet you and see your tree. I would like to buy your tree and bring it to Washington to be the country's Christmas tree for this year. I would also bring you and your family here. I would be honored if you would throw the switch that lights the tree. What do you say?"

Henry only needed to think for a second. He said, "I am very sorry, President Forrester, but I must decline your offer. My little tree is not for sale. You would have to cut it down to take it to Washington, and I want the tree to grow old with me. I would love to share the tree with the country for everyone to see its triumph and beauty, but I can't let you cut it down."

There was stunned silence for a few moments. President Forrester then said, "Listen, Henry, I need to go into an important meeting now. I'd like to talk to you again, and you have a few days to think about this. I need to fly down to Atlanta next Tuesday, and that's not too far away from you. Could you pencil me in for around two o'clock for a chat?"

Henry was happy to agree. He said. "Yes, Mr. President, that would be great! Could I ask a small favor?"

President Forrester laughed and said, "Henry, I asked to buy your tree and fly your family to Washington. I offered to let you light the tree. You said no to all three, but now you want a favor. I like your backbone and stamina, young man. Ask me the favor."

"Mr. President, it's just that no one will believe I talked to you. Would it be permissible for me to have my two best friends, Ruthie and Bruce, here next Tuesday? And could you possibly say hello to them?"

President Forrester said, "It would be my pleasure, Henry. Any friend of yours is a friend of mine." The line clicked off, and the president was gone.

The next few days went by agonizingly slow. Henry never wavered on saving the tree. It was just simply too much to think about. When Henry told Bruce and invited him over for the phone call, Bruce had sprawled on the floor laughing. Then he looked at Henry's face and realized Henry was serious. He immediately started making lists of his good clothes and charts of what he should wear. Henry continued to tell him it was just a phone call; he wouldn't see the president and the president wouldn't see him, but it was no use. Ever since Bruce had been elected to student council at school, he had believed he might have a future in politics. This would be the first step.

Ruthie was her sweet, kind, and beautiful self. She was thrilled at the invitation but didn't seem to be too fazed by it. When Tuesday finally came, Ruthie and Bruce each stayed home from school so they could look their best for the president's phone call. They arrived at Henry's at 1:00 p.m., neither wanting to take the chance the president might have to call early and they would miss their chance. Ruthie arrived in her favorite blue Sunday dress. Henry could only stammer "Hi" when she arrived. Bruce had his hair slicked back to control several cowlicks. He was wearing a navy-blue sport coat, gray slacks, white shirt, and a red tie with small American flags on it. When he arrived, Henry's reaction was "Really?" For his part, Henry had on a flannel shirt, jeans, loafers, and no socks.

It was about 1:45 p.m. when they heard a helicopter in the distance. As the noise drew closer and closer, Bruce went to the front window to look out. He didn't say anything. He just stood there with his mouth open. All of them, including Henry's mom and dad, went to the window to see what was going on. There, out in the yard, between the tree and the house, Marine One, the president's helicopter, was landing.

Bruce looked at Henry and said, "I should have worn my best clothes!"

Henry turned to him and said, "FYI, the price tags are still on the back of your pants and on your coat sleeve."

After the house had been quickly swept by the Secret Service to make sure there were no threats, President Forrester entered. He seemed very polite and was even more handsome in person. He gave each of them a firm handshake and said hello to each one as they introduced themselves. Unfortunately, Bruce could not speak. He just kept saying "Bruh...Bruh...Bruh."

Ruthie saved him. She said, "I am sorry, Mr. President. This is our friend, Bruce Champion. He can normally talk."

The president shook Bruce's hand and then turned to her. "You must be Ruthie. Thank you for helping Bruce." Ruthie gave him her thousand-watt smile and sat down.

Thankfully, Henry's mother had just made one of her home-made vanilla cream pound cakes and a pitcher of iced tea. It had been meant for after the phone call. She now offered it to all the guests, and they gladly agreed.

After everyone had been served, the president said, "Henry, since it's your tree we are talking about, how about if just the two of us go out on the porch and chat?"

It was amazing that this man, this leader of the free world, was so down-to-earth and easy to talk to. Henry stood up, said, "After you, Mr. President." And they went out to the porch.

The president sat down on the porch swing and gazed out onto the property. He said, "Although I love this weather we are having, I have to tell you, the pictures of your tree don't do it justice. It is truly spectacular, especially knowing how it looked in the beginning when you got it. I don't know whether you saw it or not, but I had our pilot make one long slow pass around the tree before we landed. Everyone on board was nearly speechless with its beauty. I need to have that tree, your family and friends, and your story come to Washington. It's a story and a symbol that our nation needs to see and hear about."

Henry said, "Thank you *so* much, Mr. President, but as I've already told you…"

The president held up his hand and said, "Hold on just a minute, Henry. Hear my 'new and improved' offer before you give me your answer." With that, he reached into his coat pocket and pulled out a folded sheet of stationery. When he opened it, Henry saw the presidential seal. President Forrester said, "This offer has three parts for you to consider. Let's talk about the tree first. Please wait until I have finished all three parts before you reply. Okay, part one. I want your tree in Washington before the holidays to display. I want your family and friends there to tell the story and celebrate. You would love to share it but don't want it cut down. I have talked to every forestry expert my staff and I could find. We can bring special equipment onto your property that can dig up the tree and its root ball intact. The experts don't recommend transporting it by railcar due to possible damage. I have reached out to several of my friends in both cargo shipments and construction. They own HALO helicopters that can hoist and carry forty-four thousand pounds apiece. Your tree has been estimated to weigh no more than forty thousand pounds. I will have *two* HALO helicopters here on the day of excavation to lift it out of the hole and carry it away. All the experts tell me there will be zero stress on the tree. I will have two dump trucks full of fill dirt standing by to fill in the large hole and a crew to smooth it over. After Christmas, we will bring the tree back and put it back the way we found it, no damage at all. Secondly, I have had my staff look over your test scores and grades. They are terrific, just as I expected. What are your plans for college?"

Henry said, "I have no plans, Mr. President. My family cannot afford to send me, and although I have looked into scholarships, there doesn't seem to be anything I qualify for. Ruthie wants to go to the University of Florida and study business and education. There's no reason to even apply. I cannot go there or anywhere."

The president smiled and said, "Henry, you are the type of student we need in the universities of this great nation. I have talked to one of my best friends about you. Although he wants to remain anonymous, he will underwrite your complete college education with no strings attached. All you have to do is get in."

By this time, Henry was just trying not to cry.

The president said, "And lastly, Henry, we come to you. I have previously talked to your parents and gotten their permission to offer you one more thing. I know you are a brave, selfless, and courageous young man. You lift everyone up and face every challenge head on. You never waiver in your determination and beliefs. There is one thing, though, that has prevented you from being all you can be. It is your crooked leg. Your parents gave your doctor permission to share the x-rays he has taken over the years of your leg. My experts at Walter Reed Hospital, where I am treated, have 100 percent confidence that they can operate on you and, with six months of physical therapy, your leg and everything having to do with your leg will be perfectly normal. A different friend of mine has said, after hearing your story, that he will pay for everything. There will never be any obligation of any kind for you to ever pay him back. What do you say, Henry?"

Henry had tears in his eyes as he looked back at the big glass window that looked into the great room. Standing side by side, with their arms around one another, were his mother and father and Ruthie with smiles on their faces but tears running down their cheeks. Crying the hardest but smiling the biggest was his lifelong friend, Bruce, who stood beside them and simply held a big piece of poster board. On the poster, he had written in big letters "Take the Deal!"

Henry smiled and said, "I accept your deal, Mr. President, but I would like to ask you for one more favor."

President Forrester had no idea what Henry could possibly ask for. He said, "We are stretched pretty thin here, Henry. What's the favor?"

Henry said, "When the tree comes back, I want it planted down where you turn onto our property. When I first got it, I planted it closer to the house so that I could keep an eye on it and take care of it. Now that it's so big, I want it planted where all my friends down in the valley can see it. I want them to see what is possible with a little love and kindness. That tree has changed tremendously, and because of it, and you, my life will be changed forever."

The president said, "Done! Let's shake on it."

As they shook hands and smiled at each other, the president knew that knowing this young man, his friends, and family would also alter his life from this day forward.

(Many, many years later, after President Forrester had passed away, Henry would learn from the president's biographer that it was President Forrester himself that had personally paid for Henry's surgery, physical therapy, and college education.)

Mom, Dad, Bruce, and Ruthie all came out onto the porch to be with them. There were many handshakes, hugs, and smiles.

The president said, "I have to go…you know, run the country and all that." He patted Bruce's shoulder and said, "I really like your tie, Bruce!"

Bruce reacted so quickly, yanking his tie off to give to the president, that three cowlicks sprang up on his head. President Forrester smiled, took the tie, and walked to his helicopter. As he reached the top step, before the blades had started to spin, he stopped, looked back at the small group, waved, and said, "It has been my sincere honor to be with each of you today. We will send details very soon to get this all started." He walked inside and was gone. Marine One started up, the blades spinning faster and faster, and lifted off into the sky.

There was a flurry of activity over the next several weeks, both phone calls and text messages. Henry and the president spoke several times. The president really wanted Henry to have his surgery and recover before the tree was taken to Washington. He wanted Henry to be completely healed and participate in all the festivities. They agreed that Henry would have his surgery, do his physical therapy, and the tree would be flown to Washington the following year.

The months flew by, and the following March, Henry entered Walter Reed Hospital to have his surgery. His family and friends stayed with him throughout the day. That night, after visiting hours were over, he heard hushed voices and quite a few people walking down the hall. The footsteps stopped outside his door. His door slowly opened, but only one person came in.

President Forrester walked over to the bed and said, "How are you doing, Henry?"

Henry said he was a little anxious, but he was also excited about his future. President Forrester told him that was completely normal. He said he was sorry he had come so late, but it always created a lot of commotion when he came to the hospital. He said he would be out of the country for the next few days at a European summit. He had come to tell Henry he knew the surgery would be a great success. He would be praying for Henry's rapid recovery and strength. He said he would be in touch, shook Henry's hand, and left.

The next day, the surgery turned out to be a spectacular success. The team of doctors told Henry's family and friends they were amazed at how well it had gone. The president called in the afternoon and offered congratulations to all. He said he was thrilled to hear of the success, not only for Henry's sake, but also it would have been "a shame to fire all those guys after the esteemed careers they had enjoyed." Everyone laughed.

Henry was sent home to begin physical therapy and homeschooling. He would not be able to attend school the last few months, but by the time summer was over, everyone hoped he would go back to school for his junior and senior years.

The therapy was long and hard, but every day Henry did his part. He pushed himself harder and harder to be as strong as he could be. The puddles of sweat around him each day attested to his efforts.

September came. When Mom, Dad, and Henry pulled up to the entrance, there was a huge crowd outside. It looked like the whole school was outside. Henry couldn't help but wonder what was going on. He got out of the old truck, and as he stepped forward on his formerly crooked leg, the students began to clap and cheer. "Welcome back, Henry!" "Way to go, Henry!" "We are *so* proud!" they all shouted. Henry proudly walked forward and was completely surrounded by all his friends and teachers.

His junior year flew by. He and Bruce began working at the town's volunteer fire department. Henry also worked at the local supermarket and saved his money. He didn't want to be any more of a burden to his benefactor than he had to be. Bruce began dating a new girl at school named Patti. She was kind, sweet, pretty, and had a great personality. She was perfect for Bruce. Patti and Ruthie quickly became best friends.

Now preparations to move the tree kicked into high gear. A date was picked for the team and equipment to arrive. President Forrester ran for reelection. The team, the dump trucks, ground crew, and two massive helicopters arrived. After carefully excavating around the tree, steel cables were attached to the tree. The helicopters lifted off, and the nearly fifty-foot tree was lifted free as if it had floated out of the ground. A huge tarpaulin that had been specially made for this was spread under the hovering tree and then attached to the tree all the way around so no debris would fall from the roots. The tree then was lifted up and floated away toward Washington. The ground crew and dump trucks did an awesome job. After a short while, the hole was completely filled in and smooth. Where the tree had stood, there was just a large patch of smooth dark earth.

President Forrester had won reelection and had Henry, his family, and friends (now including Patti) flown to Washington for all the holiday festivities, beginning with the lighting of the tree. There was a whirlwind of parties, lunches, dinners, and speeches. At last it was the night. Henry and his family and friends sat with the president, First Lady, and several dignitaries on a large podium. For this evening, President Forrester had worn Bruce's tie. The president gave a short but moving speech about the holidays. He gave Henry a short introduction, as by now everyone knew the story of Henry and his tree. He then asked Henry and his family and friends to come forward so Henry could light the tree.

They all came forward. The president smiled and said, "Henry, this is your tree. It always has been; it always will be. Thank you for sharing it with the United States of America. And for all those folks watching on televisions around the world. Just press this button and light it up for all to see."

Henry looked out at the huge crowd. He looked at his family and friends. He pushed the button.

The crowd truly gasped. Even Henry was stunned. It was truly spectacular and way more than he had ever imagined. The crowd started cheering. Henry looked at his loved ones gathered around him. They all were smiling and crying at the same time. With a great surge of emotion, he turned, closed his eyes, and kissed Ruthie. When he opened his eyes, she was smiling at him and saying, "I've been waiting so long for you to do that!"

The next day, pictures were all over the Internet, the television, and soon the magazines. There were many great pictures of the ceremony and the tree lighting. The one picture that nearly every story started with was Henry kissing Ruthie with the president of the United States standing off to their right, smiling and clapping.

True to his word, after the holidays, Henry's tree was flown home and planted exactly where Henry wanted it. The president flew Henry and his loved ones to Washington for the inauguration and parties.

Henry, Ruthie, Bruce, and Patti were inseparable throughout their senior year. Henry went out for the basketball team and made it. His ability to run and play the game were a testament to his surgery's success. He filled out and grew strong. Each one had a touch of senioritis, but each one wanted to finish strong. College applications were filled out and mailed. Ruthie had convinced them all to apply to the University of Florida. After many weeks of waiting, they all received letters from UF. They gathered together to open them. Each one slowly opened their own letter, read it, and slowly turned to look at the expression on one another's face. There was nothing but smiles. They had all been accepted. The foursome would be headed to Gainesville together.

The four years at UF were wonderful years for all of them. Ruthie majored in business and minored in education. Patti became a voice major due to her beautiful voice and vocal range. Bruce became a political science major. On his resume, under references, he listed James Forrester, President of the United States. Henry majored in English with a minor in forestry.

Even though they saw each other regularly at school, when they came home for holidays or summer, they were always together. Bruce helped the village mayor run for reelection and win. He and Henry continued to work with the volunteer fire department. Henry also continued to work for the supermarket as often as he could. They often reminisced about their special Christmas in Washington.

When they all came home for the Christmas holidays in their senior year, something was up with Henry. He seemed distracted. He seemed to spend long periods of time at his secret place on the property. As the weeks passed, the fire department's hook-and-ladder truck often went by the house and bounced down the trail that led to his secret place, filled with Henry and his firemen friends.

Although Henry, his family, friends, and nearly everyone he knew went to church on Christmas Eve, this year he said he couldn't go. He said he had work he needed to do. He asked Ruthie to come to his house after church, around 8:00 p.m. He wanted her to see something. She said, "But it will be dark. Can't I see it now?" He said she would have to wait.

She got to his house, along with his parents, right at eight. The front lights were on, but Henry didn't seem to be around. There were lights on in the barn, but if Henry was there, they didn't want to ruin the surprise. After a bit, they heard jingle bells. They all went to the front window to see what was happening.

There was an old-fashioned sleigh in the driveway being pulled by a beautiful Clydesdale horse. The sleigh was covered with tiny white twinkle lights. And everywhere it was possible, Henry had attached jingle bells. Henry stood by the horse, dressed up as if going to church.

As they came out of the house, Ruthie said, "Oh, Henry…it's so beautiful."

Henry took her hand and helped her up into the sleigh. "This isn't what I wanted you to see. You have to wait."

They trotted off under a million twinkling stars. Although covered with lights, the sleigh didn't illuminate much. She couldn't see more than three or four feet around the sleigh. They casually chatted as Ruthie snuggled up against him. For a while she could see thousands of stars, but then it seemed they were traveling into a cave. Somehow it seemed close, and all she could see were stars straight overhead. After a bit, Henry stopped. He said, "I've got to get out here for just a minute, but you stay in the sleigh. You will be fine." He walked away and was gone. After a few minutes, he called out to her. "Where I was sitting, I left a small metal box. Can you find it?"

She felt around and located the box. She called, "I have it."

Off to her right, Henry said, "Inside the box is a button. Count to ten and press the button."

She had never counted to ten so quickly in her life. She pressed the button.

Around her was a clearing. Around the clearing and back down the track they had ridden in on, thousands of Christmas lights blinked on. They illuminated the hundreds of trees that Henry had planted from the little tree's pine cone seeds. It was truly exquisite. She couldn't believe what she was seeing. This was what Henry and his friends had been using the fire department's truck and ladders for. She turned to look at Henry, but he was no longer standing there. He was down on one knee, holding a small black velvet box that held a diamond ring. He said, "Ruthie, I have loved you since the first time I saw you, since third grade. Will you marry me and make me the luckiest man alive?"

As Henry stood up, she leaped into his arms with tears running down her cheeks and hugged him tightly. "Is that a yes?" he asked with a smile on his face.

"Oh, yes, Henry, yes, yes, yes!" she said. "I have one favor to ask."

Henry quirked his eyebrow and said, "Anything."

She said, "This place is so beautiful, and the clearing is just perfect. When we get married, could we be married here in *our* secret place?"

Henry said, "I was wondering if you might like to do that. Press the button again."

When she did, the Christmas lights disappeared and were replaced by millions of white twinkle lights. It was even more beautiful and magical. It was like a fairy tale, and she was the princess.

She said, "Oh, Henry, I'm going to love you longer than forever."

Henry smiled and said, "Not as much as I am going to love you."

*****

Grandma's voice had gotten wistful as she said this last part. Daisy the goldendoodle came over, put her front paws on Grandma's lap, and looked up to her face. Grandma scratched her head and said, "It's okay, Daisy. I'm okay. Just a little sad."

Sebastian said, "That's really a special dog, isn't she, Grandma?"

Grandma said, "Yes, she is. Your granddaddy and I have had many dogs over the years. Our first Christmas, after we were married, he gave me a goldendoodle. I loved that dog so much. When we found out that Granddaddy was sick and that he wasn't going to recover, he brought this goldendoodle puppy home to me to keep me company. He didn't want me to be alone. Daisy has been great for me."

Alexandria said, "Okay, Grandma, tell us the rest of the story please."

Grandma said, "It's late. We all need to get to bed. That story will keep. Now go wash your faces, brush your teeth, put on your nightclothes, and get in bed. I will come in and kiss each of you good night."

They all got up, stretched, and headed to the bathrooms.

Grandma and Daisy went through the house, turning off lights. She let Daisy out to do her business one last time. Daisy came back in, and she locked the door. The last light to turn off was by the front glass window. She looked at the tree in the distance, lights and star shining brightly. Henry had been right. You could see the tree's lights and star down in the village. A beacon of strength, a testament of love and kindness, an example of what could happen if you tried your hardest.

She said, "Thank you, little tree, for all you have done for each of us. Shine on, little tree, shine on." She turned off the light and went to kiss the grandchildren.

The Main Event

Henry and Ruthie were amazed at how much love everyone showed them. Whether they were strolling down the streets in the village, accepting deliveries at the farm, even grocery shopping, they were greeted with back pats, hugs, big smiles, and shouts of congratulations. Word of Henry's proposal had gotten as far as possible (he thought). Their friends and family had told everyone the great news.

They were actually at the grocery store, getting ready to check out, when Ruthie turned and said, "Uh oh."

Henry asked, "What?"

She could only point. There by the checkout line was the assortment of national tabloids. The huge picture on the first one was Henry kissing Ruthie at the Christmas tree lighting. The headline read "The Christmas Tree Kid Pops the Question." The next tabloid had that picture beside a candid picture of Ruthie smiling. That headline said, "Ruthie says Yes!" Under that, it said, "The Christmas tree blessings continue."

Everyone around them was smiling and cheering as they watched Henry and Ruthie see their tabloid pictures for the first time. Henry could actually feel his face and ears turning red. They thanked everyone, quickly paid for the groceries, and headed to Henry's house to prepare his parents.

They all talked throughout the afternoon. Henry's father felt like that was as far as the news would go. He was pretty sure those tabloids had regional coverage, so the news probably wouldn't cause the uproar Henry was concerned about. Henry and Ruthie had wanted their "wedding among the trees" to be a small and intimate gathering with only close friends and family.

(A few weeks prior, one of the special education teachers at the elementary school had left on maternity leave. Ruthie had minored in education and had focused on special-needs children. She applied for the job and was quickly accepted. The job would help her save money for her dress. In order to save money, they had agreed to have the reception back at the farm outside. Hopefully, the weather would cooperate.)

The next day, she had all her students gathered around her for story time. There was a mixture of walkers, crutches, and wheelchairs. The one thing they all shared was a huge smile as Ruthie read to them. The phone rang. Ruthie made it a point to never answer the phone when she was involved with "her children." If it was important, the office would let her know over the intercom, and she would answer. The phone stopped ringing after a few more times. Ruthie continued with her story.

The phone began to ring again. The phone ringing wasn't that abnormal. Parents sometimes called and left messages about upcoming meetings, or asking if they could observe, or offering to supply treats. One father came as often as she asked, dressed up as Bubbles the Clown. He would sing, dance, and make balloon animals for the kids. They loved him! Ruthie had a *huge* heart and would do anything for those kids. At last, the phone stopped ringing.

After a few minutes, she heard the familiar click of the intercom line. She stopped reading, turned toward the speaker, and said "Yes?"

Mr. Schneider, the school principal, called out, "Ms. Priest, can you take a phone call right now?"

She answered, "Is it important? I am doing story time right now, and I don't want to ruin these moments with the students. Can the person leave a message and I will call them back in a few minutes?"

Mr. Schneider cleared his throat and, in a very important-sounding voice, said, "It's the president of the United States, President Forrester." The students started laughing and clapping as she ran to pick up her phone.

Ruthie grabbed the phone and, barely managing to seem relaxed, said, "Hello?"

The male voice on the other end of the line said, "Hold for one minute, please."

Almost immediately, she heard the president's familiar voice. "Hello, Ruthie! I hope I'm not interrupting anything too important! I understand Henry finally got around to popping the question. Even more importantly, my sources tell me you said yes. I just wanted to call and offer you my wife's and my most heartfelt congratulations! The time I have spent around you, Henry, and your families has been a true blessing to both of us. The selfless love that you and Henry share with each other *and* with all those you meet is truly magnificent."

Ruthie could only whisper, "Thank you, Mr. President."

The children, who were normally noisy when she wasn't keeping them occupied, all sat peacefully, quietly watching her.

The president continued, "Okay, well, I have to go and do some important things now, you know, running the country and all that." Ruthie laughed at the familiar line. He said, "Oh, I almost forgot! I'm sure that my wife and I will be on the invitation list since I'm the one who got Henry to take the first step." He laughed loudly here. Ruthie just gulped. "What time of year are you thinking about?"

Ruthie said, "I think in the fall, but before it gets too cold."

The president said, "Okay, great! That will be perfect!"

Ruthie kind of stammered, "Perfect for what?"

The president said, "As you know, this is my last year in office. I would like to fly my immediate family down for your wedding on Air Force One. It would be our last time together on that airplane. It would be even more meaningful if our trip was to be at your wedding."

Ruthie could only say, "Uh, okay…"

The president laughed. "One more thing…"

Ruthie asked, "There's more?"

The president said, "Just one more thing, and this will be the best for you, but also maybe the hardest to agree to."

Ruthie thought to herself, *That would be impossible!*

The president said, "I've met both your families, your friends, and even a few townspeople there. Everyone was great. You guys all share so much compassion and love for one another. One thing I know that you don't have is a lot of money. You and Henry are just starting out, and neither of your parents can give you the reception a celebration of the special love you share deserves. Please, *please*, as the First Family's gift to you, let us pay for your reception. It won't be a strain or anything. I have a lot of important friends that would love to help. I was thinking of having it back at the farm…Ruthie, are you there?"

Ruthie had needed to sit down. She answered, "But, Mr. President…"

He said, "Ruthie, please."

Ruthie finally answered, "Okay."

The president said, "Oh, Ruthie! Thanks *so* much! You have made my day! Send me the date when you decide. Bye now." He clicked off and was gone. Now all she had to do was tell Henry.

The months quickly flew by. The date was set. Bruce would be Henry's best man. His fiancée, Patti, whom everyone loved, would be the maid of honor. Because of Patti's spectacular voice, she would also sing "The Lord's Prayer" and "I Believe" during the ceremony. Ruthie's gown was long, white, and trailed behind her, shining in quiet beauty with crystals and pearls. She would wear her grandmother's long white veil, which Ruthie's mother had also worn. Patti would wear pale blue, matching both her and Ruthie's eyes. The bouquets would both be red roses and baby's breath.

The small clearing, which the trees opened up into, could hold benches and seat about eighty people, not counting the altar area and wedding bench for the couple to kneel on. Henry and his father had worked to carve the bench together. It was truly magnificent, with hearts and angels carved all around it. On Henry's side, it simply said his name. On the bride's side, he had carved hearts around the words "My forever love Ruthie." Henry's mother had made a white satin pillow for them to kneel on. Ruthie cried the first time she saw the bench.

The problem wasn't the eighty folks to sit and watch the wedding. Even with the president's family and security, there was room. The problem was going to be the reception. Now that it was known the president was coming, *everyone* wanted to come to the reception. The reasoning was always "You know, we don't have to stay. We just want to hug you guys and wish you the best." Henry knew that although he, Ruthie, and their families were well liked, the real reason was to "hang out" with the president. He was so glad they had a huge unobstructed front yard. It was large enough to fit a lot of people (he hoped). The tree at the far end would tower over the area but would still be a part of their special day!

The big day came. They had laid down pale-brown carpet tiles on the trail back to the clearing and all around that area. The trees were all a deep green, lush and beautiful. If Henry tested the lights once, he tested them fifty times! The forecast was clear and cool.

About 8:00 a.m. that day, the first of several semitrucks arrived with some equipment and things for the reception. Henry nearly had a heart attack. His mother took both his hands in hers, smiled, and said, "Now, Henry. The president is coming. That train has left the station, and it's coming. There's nothing you can do now. Don't worry about it. Enjoy your special day. Your father and I love you and Ruthie *so* very much!" She hugged him tightly. When they pulled apart, they both had tears in their eyes.

The afternoon turned to evening. Henry couldn't bear to look out in the front yard where all the work was happening feverishly. He and his family got dressed and went to their places in the clearing. As requested by Ruthie, the pathway, and all around the clearing, was lit with white twinkling lights. The clearing was illuminated by additional lights.

When it came time for the bride to enter, the music started to play. Then everyone heard jingle bells. They turned to look down the long entrance pathway. The carpet tiles had been removed and, with a huge gorgeous white horse pulling them, up the path came Henry's sleigh, covered in white twinkling lights, carrying Ruthie and her father. Henry choked up at the surprise and turned to look at his parents. His father mouthed the words, "I did it for you, Henry."

His father patted his chest over his heart three times and mouthed, "Love you, my precious son." All Henry could do was smile and try not to cry.

He turned back in time to see Ruthie's father help her out of the sleigh and the last few feet up to the altar. His heart melted at the sight of her. She was a vision of beauty. Even Bruce, beside him, whispered, "Wow!" Henry could not believe that he was going to spend the rest of his life with this beautiful creature. The words were said, songs sung, vows and rings exchanged, and at last they were pronounced man and wife. Finally, the pastor said Henry's most favorite sentence of his life (up 'til now): "You may kiss your bride." Henry pulled Ruthie to him and gave her a sweet kiss and hugged her so very hard. All he could think of was how blessed he was. Ruthie, too, felt especially blessed. As they made their way past the congregation and back down the path, Ruthie wondered how hard it was for the president's sniper team, there to protect him, to hide among the twinkle lights.

They made their way back to the reception area and were startled at the transformation. They heard music playing, but it didn't sound like the disc jockey they had hired. In place of Henry's parents' expansive front yard, there were giant white tents joined together. When they went inside, they were immediately stunned by three things.

First, there were white twinkle lights across the ceiling and down the walls. Crystal chandeliers were suspended throughout. Second, the music was from a live band—one of the most popular bands touring. Lastly, there were at least a thousand people seated at tables with white tablecloths.

The president clapped Henry on the back and said, "Well done, my friends! Congratulations!"

Henry and Ruthie were so thrilled but a little embarrassed at the grandeur. When they began to protest, he put his hands up and said, "Whoa! Whoa! Whoa! Don't worry about this. Nearly all of it was donated by my friends. It's great to have friends, as you know!" He continued, "Come over here. I need to show you something."

He made his way to the front of the tent, where the dance floor was. He said, "Look up."

There, shining down on them through a kind of ragged hole in the ceiling, was Henry's tree. Henry smiled but then looked aghast. "Oh my gosh, Mr. President! Who cut that hole?"

The president said, "I did! Well, I didn't do it. I had it done. When I got here, the tent was up and you couldn't see the tree. I told the folks that tree had been such a huge part of your life *and* your journey with Ruthie. I was sure you would want your tree to be a part of this celebration. They asked, 'What do you want us to do?' I just laughed and told them they needed to put in a big skylight." The president laughed. "I guess I'm going to have to pay for that... unless I can talk some big donor into it. Have fun, kids." And he walked away.

The evening flew by with dinner, dancing, and many speeches and best wishes. Henry and Ruthie danced as much as they could and spent the rest of the time meeting and greeting the crowd of well-wishers. Bruce spent his time at the family table, chatting with the president. Patti tried to drag him onto the dance floor as often as possible to give the president a break. At last, it was time for them to leave for the airport. They had chosen a warm, sunny place in the islands for their honeymoon.

Henry called the airport to check in. After speaking to them, he returned to Ruthie, looking very disappointed. Ruthie had been talking to Bruce and Patti, saw Henry's face, and asked, "What's the matter?"

Henry said, "There's a freak snowstorm coming up the coast. They have canceled our flight. They expect more snow to follow. It may be a few days before we can get to our hotel."

Ruthie looked devastated but put on her best smile and said, "It's okay, Henry. As long as we're together, we will be okay."

Bruce said, "Stay here for a minute" and hurried away. A few minutes later, he returned with the president.

The president said, "I heard your bad news, Henry. Let me help you and Ruthie out."

Ruthie asked, "How?"

President Forrester said, "We were going to leave about now anyway. I have to get back to Washington. How about if you and Henry hitch a ride with us and we will, um, drop you off. How about it?"

Ruthie said, "You can do that? Make an unscheduled detour like that?"

President Forrester winked at her, saying, "It's great to be president!"

Henry asked, "But what about the weather? They've grounded all normal flights."

"Aaah, Henry, but Air Force One isn't a normal plane. You have to decide quickly, because we have to go."

Henry and Ruthie looked at each other, then looked back at the president, and Henry said, "Yes, sir, thank you so much!"

Bruce smiled ecstatically and asked, "Can I go?" They all said no at the same time.

Bruce looked so dejected that the president said, "I'll tell you what, Bruce. You can come to the plane, and I will give you a fifteen-minute tour, and then you will get off. How about that?" Bruce's face lit up like he had won the lottery. He grabbed Patti, and they headed for the door.

Bruce would continue his ascent in politics for many years. One picture that was always on his desk (and on Henry and Ruthie's mantel) was a photo snapped on a snowy evening. The largest part of the picture is Air Force One. The stairs are extended down to the tarmac. Near the top of the stairs, smiling and waving, is the First Lady. A few steps down from her, also smiling and waving, are Henry and Ruthie. At the foot of the stairs is Patti, standing by Bruce and waving. Bruce is smiling but can't wave very well because he has his arm around the president like they are best friends. I have to give it to him, though. At least the president is smiling, gritted teeth or not.

The newlyweds had a great ten days on their sun-soaked vacation They talked, walked, ate, dined, enjoyed each other's company, shopped, swam, hiked to waterfalls and back, and went scuba diving. They were both tanned and still very much in love when they flew home on their commercial flight.

Life quickly returned to normal. Henry and his father had an order to first make and then carve and varnish a large dining room set including table, eight chairs, and a large serving table. They were both skilled craftsmen, making their living from creating furniture and custom-carved pieces. It was not a "get rich" occupation, but it paid the bills.

The teacher that had gone out on maternity leave decided she wanted to stay home with her baby after the delivery. Ruthie was so popular and beloved by the students and parents that the school offered her the job full time. Henry and Ruthie rented a small apartment within easy walking distance of the school. She would have to complete a few courses and get certificated in order to keep her job. She accomplished these tasks with ease.

Things went along smoothly. After their wedding, the chapel in the Christmas trees became very popular. They obviously couldn't host the lavish receptions like they had enjoyed, but that seemed to be fine with everyone. Ruthie worked full time as a teacher and booked the chapel for nearly every weekend in her spare time. She and Henry saved everything she made. They both wanted children. They also both agreed that when Ruthie had the children, she would stop working in order to stay home with them. They not only were "saving for a rainy day," but they also didn't want to get used to spending the money Ruthie was earning (knowing that sooner or later it would stop).

For their Christmas together as a couple, Henry brought Ruthie a large wrapped box with a big bow on top. The way he held the box, Ruthie couldn't see the holes he had cut into the back of the box. When she opened her present, there was a precious white curly-haired goldendoodle puppy with a pink collar. She lifted the puppy out and cuddled her.

"She's beautiful, Henry!"

Henry suggested they take her outside because she had been in the box for a while. They took her outside, and she jumped around and sniffed everything. When she came to the flower bed, she happily jumped among them, barked once, and laid down. Ruthie laughed and said, "If it's okay with you, I'm naming her Petunia!" Henry laughed and agreed.

Bruce and Patti got married. After helping the mayor for several years, when he retired, Bruce ran for and was elected as the new mayor.

After their fifth anniversary, Henry and Ruthie decided it was time to take the next step. They had plenty of love to share and were ready to have children.

Unfortunately, things don't always work out as you planned them. Two years went by, but there were no pregnancies. They began to get concerned. They went to a fertility specialist for a while. No results. Henry was tested. Nothing was wrong with him. Ruthie went through a battery of tests over a time. The last test gave them the answer they had been dreading. Ruthie would be unable to conceive. There was nothing that could be done. She could not become pregnant. They thanked the doctor for his time and went home devastated.

They cried alone and on and off together for a few days. Finally, they were able to talk about the situation. They had several long and anguished discussions. They agreed that they both still wanted children very much, maybe now more than ever. They agreed to go back to her doctor, finish the paperwork, and tell him they wanted to start adoption proceedings. They held hands and prayed that if God would not give them a baby of their own, He would allow them to adopt a child he would lead them to. They made their doctor's appointment for the following month. Life returned to normal as they waited to tell the doctor their decision.

One day, a few weeks later, Henry asked Ruthie, "Have you done something different with your hair?"

She smiled and said, "No, why?"

He said, "I don't know, you just seem different to me."

Over the next few weeks, Henry started waking up each morning, rushing into the bathroom, and throwing up. "Must be some kind of virus," he said.

Getting ready to leave one morning, he asked, "Have you changed your lipstick color or makeup?" Again, she said no. It was clear that she was aggravated when Henry asked her these questions. Plus, Henry was still throwing up every morning. He decided to stop asking and just lay low…but he knew something was happening to her.

The night before their doctor's appointment, she was unusually sad, dredging up all the sad memories from their last visit. Henry, on the other hand, was wired. He couldn't sit still, pacing from room to room. When they went to bed, he thrashed around in the bed, unable to sleep. At long last, around 3:00 a.m., lying there sweaty and exhausted, he heard a voice beside him speak. Not only was it a masculine voice, but it was on the opposite side of Henry, away from Ruthie. The voice simply said, "It's okay, Henry. Ruthie is pregnant." He completely relaxed and went to sleep. When he woke in the morning, he wondered whether he had been dreaming.

The doctor called them into the office and sat down, smiling at them. He said he was so relieved they had returned and seemed to be coping with their situation. He was happy to help them with the adoption process. Henry, who had been fidgeting the whole time, couldn't take it anymore. He said, "Dr. Young, you are going to think I am crazy, but I have to tell you. I think Ruthie is pregnant!"

Ruthie put her head in her hands and started to cry. The doctor said, "Henry, don't do this to you or Ruthie. Look how upset she is. I know you are churning and upset inside, but the truth is she cannot be pregnant. It's totally impossible." Henry wouldn't change his mind. The doctor finally said, "Okay, let's do this. Let's put off our adoption talk until next month. Neither of you are ready to do this. Secondly, Ruthie, would you consent to giving us samples to test if you are pregnant? That way, Henry will know." Ruthie tearfully agreed.

They left the doctor's office after being told the test would take four to five hours. Henry said he would call at 2:00 p.m. He drove Ruthie to work, walked her to class, kissed her goodbye, and left.

The day dragged on. Henry was now working on a living room table for a client. At 2:00 p.m. sharp, he called the doctor's office. He asked for their favorite nurse. She got on the phone and confessed that she had not called the lab for the results. She said Ruthie and Henry were their favorites, and no one wanted to get results that would hurt them…again.

Henry said, "I'm telling you…I *know* she's pregnant! Just make the call." She put the phone down and picked up another line. Henry heard her identify herself and then ask for lab results for a patient… last name "Taggart," first name "Ruthie." He heard her kind of squeal and then say, "Are you sure?" When she picked Henry's line up again, he heard other nurses too. It sounded like some were laughing and some were crying. She said, "How did you know?" All Henry said was "Gotta go." He hung up the phone and ran out the door.

He went to the drugstore, looking for something specific, quickly located it, and paid. He found a small box for it and wrapped it in the parking lot. He tied a ribbon around the package, put a bow on it, and drove to the school. School was out for the day, so he went straight to Ruthie's class. When she turned around and saw him, she saw the package. Henry was crying, and she completely misread the situation. She sat down, crying, and he handed her the small package. She opened the package, and there was a small package with four diaper pins in it. Each little pin had a smiling happy duck on it.

Ruthie turned to Henry and said, "I don't understand."

Henry took her hand and said, "Don't lose those. You're going to need them in nine months. You are going to have our baby and be a mommy!"

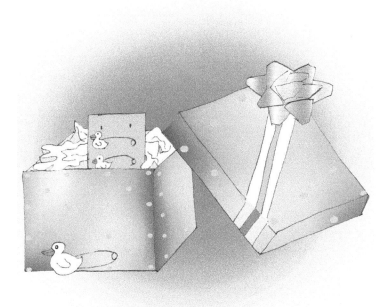

Henry began to work feverishly. A little over nine months later, their precious Amanda was born happy, healthy, and completely normal. By that time, Henry and his father had carved a crib, cradle, bassinet, and changing table. Obviously, Bruce and Patti became Uncle Bruce and Aunt Patti.

A year flew by. Ruthie continued to see her doctor, who was continually amazed. He said, "Be very careful. I cannot begin to imagine or predict how easy or hard it will be for you to become pregnant again, or if ever."

On Amanda's first birthday, in February, Henry said, "Let's start trying again. I know God really blessed us the first time, but it might be harder this time. You and I have both said we want our children to be born within a few years of each other so they can have things in common and grow up together." Ruthie said she completely agreed.

Their precious son, Adam, was born ten months later in December. Uncle Bruce and Aunt Patti were thrilled!

Bruce's political star continued to rise. At first grudgingly, but later with respect and at least a little love, President Forrester had guided Bruce and introduced him to all the right people. In 1980, at the ripe old age of thirty-four, Uncle Bruce Champion was appointed lieutenant governor of the state. Eight years later, he ran for and was elected governor. Henry, Ruthie, and both children were guests of honor at his inauguration. Prior to his first Thanksgiving as governor, after a *lot* of haggling with Henry, Uncle Bruce had the state purchase two of Henry's trees. One went to the governor's mansion, and the other went to the state capitol building.

(The media all wondered if this was a sign. Would Bruce Champion one day run for the presidency? After all, Forrester was his mentor, and Forrester had had to return Henry's tree. Governor Champion had bought two trees *and* had them planted. They weren't going back.)

Amanda loved her little brother fiercely. She wanted to help Ruthie with every task that pertained to Adam. Her favorite was picking out his attire for the day. He was her living, breathing baby doll, and she adored him.

Around the age of two years old, Adam got very sick. The doctors all thought it was the flu, as that was going around. Adam didn't get better. He became more and more pale. When the doctor saw him the next time, he was very concerned over how pale he appeared and immediately ran a few blood tests. When the doctor returned to the room where Ruthie, Amanda, and Adam waited, he had his two partners with him. From the looks on their faces, Ruthie knew the news must be very bad.

They told her that Adam's blood count was dangerously low. They didn't understand why he wasn't in a coma because of such a low count. They sent Ruthie and the children to the hospital where Henry met them. Late that afternoon, a surgeon came by to talk to them. He said he had reviewed the case with his colleagues. They had determined that Adam must have been bleeding internally. They recommended that two tests be performed the following morning. The tests, using radioactive isotopes, would pinpoint where the bleeding was coming from. After that, it should be a simple operation to seal off the leak. Henry and Ruthie agreed.

Henry called his parents, and Ruthie called hers. The grandparents all began to call their church friends and all of Henry and Ruthie's friends. When anyone asked what they could do, they were just asked to pray for Adam. Henry and Ruthie prayed, too, that their precious son would be okay, that God would watch over all of them.

The night was long, with not much sleep for any of them.

The next morning, the two-timed medical tests were performed. All that was left now was to wait. The day dragged on. The surgeon came back in the afternoon and was clearly frustrated. He said the tests had to be done in a specific order to give the specific information they needed. He said somehow, the two tests had been reversed and done out of order. They could retrieve no data. They would have to do the tests again tomorrow. Everyone was stunned. As he turned to leave, he stopped at the door and said, "One curious thing. Adam's last blood sample, taken an hour ago, showed his blood count was rising." He wasn't sure what that meant but said he would see them tomorrow.

The next morning, they took more blood samples and did the tests correctly. The blood sample showed Adam's blood count had risen another four points. When he had entered the hospital, he had been down nineteen points and apparently, now his body was building the count back up. The test results showed no evidence of internal bleeding. The doctor said, "We will take one more blood sample in the morning. If it has continued to rise, we will send him home." In the morning, Adam's count was up three more points, and Adam was taken home. Two weeks later, at his follow-up appointment, his blood count was back to normal. It has stayed that way all his life.

Henry's parents invited the family over for dinner one night. Grandma and Granddaddy Taggart loved having them over, especially the grandchildren! They babysat whenever they were needed (and sometimes even when they weren't needed) just to play with Amanda and Adam. They enjoyed another remarkable meal that

Grandma had fixed. Afterward, Henry cleared the table and washed and dried the dishes while everyone else went to the great room to play with the babies. Henry dried his hands and joined them.

As he sat down, he glanced over at the mantel where his three favorite pictures were. On the left was a picture of Henry and Ruthie on their wedding day. They were sitting in the sleigh. All the lights were sparkling. It was barely snowing. Ruthie looked absolutely radiant. Even the horse looked happy.

The middle picture was the six of them—Granddaddy, Grandma, Henry, Ruthie, Amanda, and Adam. It was a very simple picture, but every time Henry looked at it, his heart swelled with pride and love.

The last picture was the Air Force One picture.

Henry's father told them that he and Grandma had been talking. They had returned to the subject a number of times and always happily came to the same conclusion. He said, "Please hear me out on this." Grandma reached over and took his hand in hers. He continued, "This house has gotten too big for us. Your apartment has gotten too small for you. You know we have the caretaker's cottage that we have kept up for years, even though no one has lived there. It's a cute little three-bedroom bungalow. It's just the perfect size." Henry thought it would be perfect for him and his little family. Then Granddaddy dropped the bombshell. "Grandma and I propose that we move into the cottage and you guys move into this house. It would be doing us a great favor. We don't need all this space, and you could certainly use it. Please say yes!"

Henry and Ruthie were too stunned to speak. At last, Henry said, "Mom, Dad, this is such a generous offer! I feel like it's too much though. I don't want you to have to move out because of us."

Granddaddy said, "We don't have to. We want a smaller place. It would mean no more rent payments for you, more space for the children inside and outside, and we could see Amanda and Adam every day. Please, Henry, Ruthie, say yes. It would mean the world to us."

Henry looked at his mother. She was smiling and nodding. He looked at Ruthie. She had tears in her eyes, but she was smiling too. She said, "It's up to you, Henry. I will follow you wherever you go."

Henry looked back at his father. He took one of his dad's hands in his, shook it, and said, "We can never repay you for *all* you have done in both our lives. This is *so* huge. This house and the opportunity to raise our family here is more than I could ever have hoped for. My answer is yes."

Henry and his father worked in and around the caretaker's cottage for a little over a month, cleaning, painting, and making it perfect. Since the cottage was furnished, only a few special pieces had to be moved in. Henry and Ruthie had very few things to move. They took the master suite, put Amanda next door in her own room, and put Adam in Henry's former bedroom. Moving day ended with everyone snuggled into their new homes. All was perfect.

Time passed quickly for all of them. Amanda went to kindergarten, and then on to elementary school. Two years later, Adam entered kindergarten, and Ruthie returned to teaching special education. Amanda soon fell in love with anything having to do with horses. If it had a mane, a tail, four legs, and was breathing, she was thrilled. As she grew older, she became more and more involved, whether mucking out stalls or riding competitively, she was committed to it.

Adam soon encountered sports, and a lifelong passion for *all* sports ensued. He started playing T-ball when he was six. He considered himself the ultimate competitor. His favorites to participate in were basketball and baseball. If he had to watch sports on television, it had to be the Chicago Cubs or the Florida Gators.

Ruthie and Henry often found themselves passing each other in their cars, as one was headed to the stables and one was headed to sports practice. Weekends were often filled with either athletic competitions or horse shows. It was always a family affair, as Granddaddy and Grandma were always in the stands cheering.

The one rule that was constant with Henry and Ruthie concerned grades. If either Amanda or Adam didn't keep their grades up to what they were capable of, the extracurricular activities would immediately cease. That was the greatest motivation that either could have. They worked hard and played even harder. The grades stayed up, and so did their outside passions.

Amanda was polite and popular, dating a number of different guys, always looking for Mr. Perfect. Henry regularly pointed boys out to Amanda and said, "See that guy. Don't be bringing someone like him home. He will never treat you like a princess, with respect and love, like Mom and I have treated you." He could only hope she listened to him.

Adam started dating Carrie when she was in tenth grade and he was in twelfth. It was clearly apparent that theirs was not a passing fancy. Although both dated others from time to time, it was obvious they would one day end up with each other.

Amanda applied to and was accepted at the University of Florida. She was approved for summer term and began taking classes three weeks after her high school graduation. Adam was *so* jealous that he had to wait two more years to go there. He took a little more time with his studies, wanting to make sure his grades were good enough to get him in. At last, it was time to apply. He sent the completed application in and then waited…and waited…and waited. He walked down the long driveway to the big Christmas tree, Daddy's tree, to check the mailbox each day. He would walk back dejectedly every day, carrying the mail but nothing from UF.

As luck would have it, on the day this special letter came, he was at baseball practice at the high school. Ruthie was on the way to pick him up and stopped by the mailbox. She saw the UF logo and, although she knew Adam should be the one to open the letter, she couldn't take the suspense. She tore the envelope open, quickly scanned the letter, jumped back in her idling car, and raced all the way to the school. She parked by the field and ran down the fence line, first base side, waving the letter. Adam saw his mother frantically waving the letter, and even before he noticed the familiar orange and blue logo, he realized what it must be. He looked to the coach, who was grinning at him. The coach said, "Go see." And Adam sprinted to the fence.

Adam knew when he got there and saw his mother's face and the torn envelope what the letter said. He still had to read it for himself. Ruthie passed it through the chain-link fence. Adam read the letter, looked back at Ruthie, and said, "I made it! I'm going to be a Gator! I'll be with Amanda at the school that you, Dad, Uncle Bruce, and Aunt Patti all attended! I can't believe it." He ran around the fence, grabbed his mother, and hugged her tightly. He wasn't even mad that she had opened the letter first.

The days passed and, at summer's end, the four of them drove to Gainesville, Florida. Amanda considered herself a pro by this time and didn't think her father and mother needed to come. Ruthie, however, felt it would be a great family trip. Also, she wanted to make sure her son had everything he needed before she left him. After two days in Gainesville and many trips to the grocery store (food), Target (linens), campus bookstore (books), and the Gator Shoppe (Gator tees and supplies), it was time to leave for home. Henry and Ruthie took them both to lunch. Afterward, they all hugged one another tight and said their goodbyes. Henry opened the car door for Ruthie, and she got in. He closed the door, went around, and climbed in behind the steering wheel. He turned to look at both the kids. He patted his chest over his heart three times, like his father had taught him, and pointed at each of them. They each smiled and made the same gesture back at him and Ruthie. He started the car and headed home.

Henry and Ruthie settled into their new lives, just the two of them again. The kids came home for Christmas break. They had brought tons of stories and laughter, even though they talked on the phone several times per week. They also brought home more dirty laundry than Ruthie could believe.

All of them had a great Christmas break. Grandma and Granddaddy came to the house every day, where they all shared stories, meals, and even made cookies. The first cookie Ruthie made, which would eventually become Amanda's favorite, was a candy cane cookie. It had two strips of dough (one was red, one was white) twirled together and shaped like a candy cane. Crushed peppermint candies were sprinkled on top.

Christmas day came, and it had snowed the night before. The yard was covered, and even the trees had been lightly dusted. Grandma and Granddaddy came over early for a special breakfast Ruthie had made. Henry got a roaring fire going. After eating as much as they possibly could of the cinnamon streusel coffeecake, eggs, and bacon, they adjourned to the great room to open gifts.

There were many wonderful gifts exchanged: sweaters, Gator hats, Gator sweatshirts, pants, shirts, etc. The highlight of the gift giving was the gifts Henry had made for each of them. He had carved a beautiful heart-shaped box for Ruthie. When she opened it up, a tiny music box played "I Will Always Love You." His mother received a carved box with his, Ruthie's, Amanda's, and Adam's faces carved into it. When she opened hers, the tiny music box played "I Believe" from her wedding. His dad also received a carved box. Carved into it were images of the crutches he had lovingly carved for Henry. Around the crutches were hearts. It played "Wind beneath My Wings."

Amanda's box was carved with galloping horses and played "I Can't Smile without You." Lastly, Adam's box was carved with the figures of Albert and Alberta, the Gator mascots. There were also footballs and baseballs. Inside the lid was carved his baseball jersey no. 44. It played the UF Alma Mater.

Winter break ended, and the kids went back to school with the car packed with everything they had brought, including clean clothes and more than enough goodie bags for the trip back. They promised to return in less than three months for spring break.

Another summer came, another Christmas passed. Carrie was now at UF, and she and Adam were exclusive. In this, her senior year, Amanda had actually found her Mr. Perfect. His name was Dennis, and he was majoring in building construction. Ruthie and Henry could only hope that Amanda would end up with Dennis and Adam would end up with Carrie. Henry and Ruthie prayed that their children would marry spouses that loved them as much as they loved each other.

Amanda graduated from UF and came home to work with the family business. The business had grown to the point that they needed someone full time to help with getting Henry's carvings shipped out to clients, booking the weddings, and dealing with all the phone calls. After Governor Champion, Uncle Bruce, had installed her daddy's Christmas tree outside his governor's mansion, her father's huge trees got even more publicity. There were calls from all over the country wanting to purchase one. Henry would only sell five per year, as he didn't want to deplete the stock.

Amanda decided they needed a brand. She had taken both art and advertising courses at UF. After *many* hours of thinking and sketching, she came up with a logo she really liked. She had taken the first letter of the words "Henry and Ruthie Taggart." That spelled HART. She replaced the *A* with a Christmas tree. Lastly, that Christmas tree was silhouetted against a red heart. She showed the drawing to her brother and parents. Everyone agreed that it was perfect. From then on, the trees that were shipped were always shipped from the HART Tree Farm.

Dennis came secretly to Henry and Ruthie to ask for their permission to marry Amanda. They were thrilled and enthusiastically agreed. Amanda said yes. They had a beautiful wedding and reception. They left the reception in a beautiful carriage pulled by two magnificent horses. The horses were from a local farm where Amanda spent her spare time riding.

Adam graduated from UF. Shortly afterward, he proposed to Carrie. (She had one year left at UF.) She also accepted. Their wedding date would be shortly after her graduation.

Adam returned home and went into homebuilding, just as Dennis had at a different company. They both loved their jobs and were good at them.

One day, while Carrie was home on spring break, she and Adam went with Amanda and Dennis to ride around the tree farm on ATVs. They came to the familiar T where, if you turned right, you went to the HART Christmas tree chapel. Amanda, however, turned left on the road that led down to a large lake on the property. They got there just as the sun was beginning to descend behind the trees at the far end of the lake.

The sky was lit up in shades of pink, orange, yellow, and blue. The reflection on the lake was truly breathtaking. As they stopped and dismounted, Amanda said, "I've been having an idea that I wanted to run by you guys. I haven't even told Mom and Dad." They looked at her expectantly and waited. She continued, "What if we built a dock out into the water? At the end of the dock would be a large stationary platform. A pergola-type roof would cover the platform."

Adam smiled and asked, "For white twinkling lights?"

Amanda laughed and said, "Yes, we could put railings on the dock for additional effect and safety. We could grade the area leading up to the dock and have seating that could be illuminated there. Can you imagine getting married with that sunset as the backdrop?"

Carrie had a huge smile and said, "Yes, I can!"

Carrie and Adam were the first to be married at the new HART Chapel on the lake. The sunset and ceremony were truly perfect.

Keys to the Future

Both Henry and Ruthie agreed. Their lives were truly blessed.

Both couples—Amanda and Dennis, and Adam and Carrie—had bought homes not far from the tree farm. They saw each of them nearly every day. Amanda, and now Carrie, were helping out more and more with the business. Adam had started helping Henry to build and create furniture in his spare time. He was also just beginning to carve sculptures, but it looked like he had the gift.

Dennis was now the purchasing director at his company. He was constantly exposed to new building materials that were being used. As things grew popular, he was able to pass that information on to Henry and Adam. He was also wonderful at negotiating fair pricing on materials. He helped the HART business a great deal with that.

Adam became the land acquisition manager at his company. His job was to find large parcels of land, out of which his company could create neighborhoods and amenity centers. As he looked at these large parcels, he began to look for smaller parcels, five to ten acres, where the two couples could expand and build larger homes one day.

One thing you could count on each year was their Halloween parties. Every year since birth, Amanda and Adam had loved getting costumes and being with friends. Just because they were grown and married, they didn't think there was any need to stop this fun. Their solution was that they threw a massive Halloween costume party for all their friends and family. They alternated hosting at each other's house every year.

One night in February, they had all gathered at Henry and Ruthie's for dinner. When dinner and dessert were over, everyone gathered in the great room, as usual, to chat. Amanda turned to Carrie and Adam and said, "I know it's my turn to host our Halloween party, but I wanted to give you the heads up and tell you we won't be able to do it. I need you to do it again this year." Adam and Carrie were not only incredulous but also a little frustrated. A party like theirs took a lot of work, focus, and planning. It was okay in the past because each couple only had to do it every other year.

Adam was a little ticked off as he asked, "And why can't *you* do it?"

Amanda smiled and said, "Well, to tell you the truth, we will be having a baby right around that time. I don't think I will have time to pull the party off."

Everyone clapped, cheered, and jumped up. Ruthie nearly knocked Carrie and Henry down as she ran to hug her daughter.

The rest of the evening's mood turned to one of elation and questions: "Do you know what sex the baby is?" "What's the due date?" "What are some names you've picked?" "How long have you known?" "Why didn't you tell us?"

As everyone was preparing to leave, Amanda said, "I have one question. So, Adam and Carrie, will you do the Halloween party this year?"

Everyone laughed, and Carrie said, "Of course!"

The months went by in a blur of business, baby showers, and shopping. Amanda asked to use the crib, cradle, and table that Henry and his father had originally carved for her. She promised to keep them in perfect shape in case she, or Carrie, needed them in the future. The fact that his first grandchild would lie in the same cradle as his precious daughter, *and* that Henry and his father had created those pieces, warmed Henry's heart. He smiled and turned to wipe tears away so no one would see.

In November, precious Alexandria was born. Henry wanted to call her Pumpkin Pie. Amanda said that he had already given that name away, to her, when she was little. After some thinking, he decided to call Alexandria Pumpkin Tart. As she grew up, she loved that nickname. It was what he called her all his days.

Another spectacular year passed. Adam and Carrie hosted everyone for Christmas day. After breakfast, presents, and then a terrific lunch, Adam said he wanted to share with the family the gift Carrie had gotten him. He pulled out a large sterling silver jingle bell ornament. Everyone "oohed and aahed" as it was passed around. When it got to Ruthie, Adam said, "It's also a box, Mom. Open it up and read the note that's inside."

Ruthie unhinged the small clasp, pulled out a tiny sheet of paper, and unfolded it. As she looked at the note, she kind of gasped and said, "The note says Merry Christmas, Daddy! I love you *so* much. I can't wait to meet you. It's signed 'Your baby.'"

"Auntie Amanda" was the first person to get to Carrie and hug her this time.

They were celebrating Henry's birthday in March when Amanda shared that she, too, was expecting! The blessings just continued to make life sweeter and sweeter. In September, after the whole family had spent the night in the waiting room, Carrie gave birth to Sebastian. He was happy, healthy, and the first boy. The family, including Alexandria, loved him very much! It was a few years, but Granddaddy started writing stories about him, nicknaming him Charlie Chucklebutt.

As the days progressed toward Amanda's due date, people would ask Alexandria what they were going to name the baby. Alexandria always smiled but insisted emphatically that the baby would be named Cock a Doodle Do. Fortunately, she didn't get her way. Her sister, Genevieve, was born in November. Her nickname, fairly quickly, was Little G or just G.

Another year passed. Henry's father retired. The furniture work had gotten too strenuous for him. He decided he would just like to spend time with Henry's mother and do some fishing. He stopped by the shop every day just to check in. He always had candy in his pockets for any of the great-grandchildren that were there. He and Henry's mother would walk hand in hand out to the giant Christmas tree. They would sit on the bench that Henry had carved, just chatting with each other and any neighbors that stopped in. In the late afternoon, they would come walking back up the long driveway and head home. Henry bought them a brand-new golf cart, decorated in orange and blue. It had the Gator logo on the front. He didn't want them to have the long walk down the driveway and back.

Henry's folks were appreciative but very rarely used the golf cart. His father said they liked the exercise and the walk. The cart sat in front of their cottage for a while but was finally relegated to the garage for use whenever they needed it.

Henry's father passed away peacefully in his sleep in the early fall. Henry was heartbroken, having known and loved this man not only as his father but also his partner, his mentor, and his friend. The whole family grieved for this man, their patriarch. About four months later, Henry's mother also passed away. She had been so very lonely since her husband's death and missed him fiercely. They had been together as husband and wife for over sixty years. She had told the family countless times that she didn't think she could go on without him. She had been right.

The thing that had lifted all their spirits and lifted them from grieving was news from Carrie. She was expecting again! The last of Henry and Ruthie's grandchildren, Adelyn, was born the following December, shortly before Christmas. In the stories Granddaddy would later write about her, he nicknamed her Petunia Picklebottom.

The two families worked to convert the old caretaker's cottage into more of a nursery. After it was finished, they began an extensive search for a nanny that could come each day and keep the four children while their mothers worked. Everyone thought this was a superb idea as the children were close by, could be seen regularly throughout the day, and could grow up together, at least in the early years. After interviewing *so* many people, they all agreed on Ms. Evelyn. She was sweet, kind, took great care of the children, but most importantly, helped to teach them manners. (Even after the kids went off to kindergarten and later elementary school, she watched over them in the afternoons.) She became a lifelong friend to all of them.

Both mothers brought their children to the cottage each morning, got them settled with Ms. Evelyn, and then they headed over to the shop to work. They brought their lunches to work and, nearly every day, went over to the cottage to have lunch with the children. Ruthie also went nearly every day, and Henry came as often as possible. Not only did that give them time to play with the kids, but it also gave Ms. Evelyn time to have a little peace and quiet while she ate her lunch.

In the afternoons, especially as Alexandria and Genevieve got older, Amanda took them to the nearby farm the Whitakers owned where she worked. Amanda didn't really work there. She spent time helping out whenever she could—mucking stalls, feeding the horses, putting them in their stalls, whatever they needed. In exchange, she was able to ride the beautiful horses and compete in horse shows as often as she wished. As Alexandria got older, she helped her mother and soon had the same love for horses that her mother did. Amanda would often saddle up one of the horses late in the afternoon. One of the farmhands would lift Alexandria up to Amanda. Alexandria would be placed right in front of Amanda, and they would happily walk around the corral. The whole time, Alexandria would be laughing and clapping her little hands.

Genevieve loved to sit in the shade and draw during their rides. She always seemed to have a real eye for colors. As she got older, she was always sketching dresses, lady's coats, purses, and even boots. She always combined the colors in such imaginative and striking ways! She told everyone who asked that when she grew up, she was going to be a fashion designer and have her own store.

When Amanda turned forty, Dennis surprised her *and* fulfilled one of her lifelong dreams. He bought her a horse of her own! It was a beautiful deep-brown mare with a black mane. Her name was Azalea. Amanda and Alexandria now rode every day. Alexandria began to take lessons shortly afterward so she could also compete.

As the girls were growing up, over at Adam's house, things were going in a very different direction. Sebastian idolized his father and wanted to do everything that Adam did or had done growing up. He was swinging a baseball bat and trying to hit balls as soon as he was able. Adam spent hours softly tossing the ball and letting him practice. At age six, Sebastian joined his first T-ball team. He played as hard as he could and became just as competitive as his father was.

Sebastian also fiercely loved the Florida Gators and the Chicago Cubs just as his father did. If it was football or basketball season, and he didn't have a game of his own, everyone knew where Sebastian would be…sitting right beside his father, watching the Gators on television and cheering them on. If it was baseball season, he would be in the same spot, cheering on the Cubs! When Sebastian was in third grade, Adam took him to Chicago to see a Cubs game in person, just as Henry had taken Adam.

As they walked out of the stadium after the game, Sebastian turned to Adam and said, "You know, Dad, one day when I'm grown, married, and have children of my own, I want to bring my son to a Cub's game. I'm hoping you will come with us."

Adam bent down and hugged Sebastian tightly, saying, "I would love to come with you!"

Adelyn was perfecting her baking and cooking skills during those years. She loved working beside Carrie to make the family dinners. She was always interested in trying new recipes. As she continued to grow up, she would alter the recipes, adding a spice here, a different ingredient there, always adapting the simpler recipes to make them her own. As she grew, the recipes became more complex, but her determination always produced terrific results. Her dessert recipes and baking skills were just as good!

Back at the farm, Henry hired another man to help him with the daily jobs. This young man's name was Toby. He was a great help to Henry and worked tirelessly every day, doing what was requested and other things that he just noticed that needed to get done. He kept the small area where Amanda and Carrie parked trimmed and neat. Often, when it rained, he would walk out with a large umbrella to their cars so they didn't get wet. He was especially kind to Ruthie. The whole family loved him.

After about six months, Henry invited the family over to dinner one night. Afterward, he proposed that now that the cottage wasn't needed as a nursery anymore, they should adapt it back to being the cottage it had been. There weren't very many things that would have to be changed, mostly clean up and paint. Since Amanda and Adam had their own houses, it was Henry's idea that after this was done, he would offer it to Toby, his wife, and young three-year-old son, rent-free. The family enthusiastically agreed.

The family quickly focused on getting the cottage ready. Toby had no idea what was going on, but he was touched when one of them would ask, "What color do you like for this area?" When Toby's wife, Jackie, would stop by with their son, Brian, whoever was working on the cottage would invite her in and show her the latest improvements. She, too, was asked "What color do you like for the master bedroom or the kitchen? What about the master bath?" She felt honored. The family treated her family as if they were related.

The cottage was quickly spic and span and freshly painted. Ruthie invited Toby and his family to have dinner with all of them. This was not unusual as Toby and his family had often had casual dinners with the family.

Dinner was terrific! Adelyn had made her famous peach cobbler, and it was perfect. Toby thought it was very strange as the family continued to smile at him, Jackie, and Brian throughout the meal.

Adelyn and Genevieve were almost bouncing in their chairs. They were so excited.

Toby asked them several times, "What's up, girls?" They would always say "Nothing!" and giggle.

They cleaned up afterward and adjourned to the great room. When they had all settled into their places, Henry took Ruthie's hand, and they walked over toward Toby and his family. Henry said, "Toby, Jackie, and Brian, we have only known you for six months, but you each have endeared yourselves to us. You have worked so hard and done more than we have asked of you, Toby. Jackie, you have pitched in and helped with whatever task we needed extra help with. Little Brian, we *all* love you, especially Auntie Alexandria, Auntie Genevieve, and Auntie Adelyn." The girls all smiled.

Sebastian said, "Hey! What about me? Who got him his first baseball and bat? I love him too!" Everyone laughed, including Brian.

Henry went on. "You've helped us fix up the cottage. You must have been wondering why."

Jackie said, "Actually, Toby and I have been talking about that. We were hoping you might be preparing it to rent out. We both hoped the rent wouldn't be too high so we could rent it and be your tenants. Are you going to rent it? And if so, how much? We would love to raise our son out here."

Henry said, "We are not going to rent it."

Toby felt his smile falter. He looked at Jackie. She looked like she was going to cry.

Ruthie said, "Hurry up, Henry. Tell them!"

Henry said, "We are not going to rent it because we want your family to move in, rent-free. It will be yours as long as you want to stay here with us. What do you say?"

No one said anything. Toby and Jackie just ran to embrace Henry and Ruthie. There were cheers and tears all around the room.

High school started, and the grandchildren all found even more friends. Alexandria quickly found out she really enjoyed biology. Her love of animals, especially horses, soon turned into a passion for learning how they were made and what procedures or medicines could help them. Her passion for biology and the sciences did not slow her popularity. In her junior year, she made the varsity cheer-leading squad. In her senior year, she made captain of the cheerlead-ers and was selected as Homecoming Queen. She also applied to and was accepted at the University of Florida. She wanted to be a veterinarian.

Sebastian's high school career was also focused on the sciences, only he enjoyed scientific research. His grades remained high. He was chosen for the varsity baseball team in his tenth grade year. In his junior year, the team went to play in the state high school baseball tournament. They came in second. In his senior year, the team again played in the same state tournament. Sebastian pitched. His team won the tournament, and he was named MVP. He also applied to "the only school I'm interested in" and was accepted at the University of Florida!

Genevieve pursued anything having to do with fashion or finance, but there wasn't too much offered. She used her tablet and computer enthusiastically to keep up with trends and learn about managing money. She figured that one day, when she was making money, she would need to know how to budget even better. Not to be outdone by her sister, she, too, was a varsity cheerleader and made captain. The pressure was on in her senior year as both Alexandria and Sebastian were at UF. She came through with flying colors. She, too, applied to UF and was accepted. She would study fashion and finance.

That left Adelyn all alone in high school. Her brother and cous-ins were all off at college! What would she do? Could she survive on her own? She quickly proved to everyone that "Yes, she could!" She took home economics courses and even helped her teachers with techniques several times. She was entered in a county baking compe-tition and a state baking competition. She won both. In her senior year, she competed in her school's beauty pageant and was crowned Miss Bartram Trail when she won.

She wanted desperately to keep the legacy alive. Her grandpar-ents, Auntie Amanda, and Uncle Dennis, even her parents, brother, and *both* cousins went to the University of Florida. Now came the waiting part. She applied to and was accepted at UF. She would take general studies but hoped to one day attend a cooking school overseas.

They all saw each other often, both on and off the campus. They studied together, partied together, and often drove back home together. Typically, if one of them was somewhere, the other three weren't far away.

They came home as often as possible throughout the year. In the summers, they all had favorite jobs that they returned to every year. Alexandria worked at the Whitaker's horse farm that her mother had taken her to when she was just a toddler. The owners were getting older and especially appreciated her help whenever she was available. She just loved being with the horses. The owners had recently bought a matched pair of warmblood horses that were truly magnificent. Annabelle was a chestnut brown with a white star, white stockings, and a black mane. Marie was a black-and-white piebald. Not only were they beautiful, but they also seemed to love Alexandria as much as she loved them.

Sebastian returned each year to his job as an intern at the TRI County Laboratory. It was twenty miles from the tree farm and was doing cutting-edge technology in many fields. Sebastian was able to divide his time between the different areas, helping him decide where he wanted his career to go.

Genevieve worked in a ladies' fashion store downtown. The owner had recognized G's talents and abilities early. Consequently, she had taken G under her wing, often letting her design the layout that would be in the front window and dress the mannequins. Her windows were always bright, colorful, and seemed professional.

Adelyn had found this cute French bistro that she loved. She went to work there and was quickly promoted to head pastry chef. Her designs, and what she could do with whipped meringue, were magnificent.

All the grands were not only doing well in school but had also found homes for their careers. It is said that if you find something you love to do and get paid for it, you never have to work. Henry and Ruthie knew that was true of their grands. They were so pleased and proud!

Henry and Ruthie were going to celebrate their fiftieth wedding anniversary in just a few months. The whole family joined together to plan out a beautiful and wonderful celebration of their love. The grandchildren called in regularly to offer their suggestions. Even the music, going all the way back to some of their favorite Elvis Presley tunes, was carefully selected. They were all *so* excited about how this party was coming together!

What the family didn't know was Henry and Ruthie were planning a huge surprise of their own. This was going to be a shocking revelation for the family. They had talked about this *so* much and had planned and planned. They were both wheeling and dealing in secret. They often looked at each other and grinned, just thinking about it and the way the family would react. Everything seemed to be working out perfectly for the surprise!

Over the next two months, Henry started experiencing quite a bit of pain. He attributed it to old age and said his body parts weren't up to snuff since their warranties had expired. As the party drew closer, everyone grew more and more excited. Henry and Ruthie secretly went to a doctor and a specialist to see what was causing the pain.

They were not prepared for the news. The specialist confirmed the diagnosis of Henry's family doctor. Henry had cancer. It had metastasized and was throughout his body. Henry didn't have much time left.

Henry managed to ask, "How much time?"

The specialist answered, "I am *so* sorry! Your doctor has shared with me just how very special your family is and how much you are loved. I don't think you have much time left at all, maybe two months, but more likely one month or so. I can give you medicine to keep you comfortable."

Ruthie was seriously crying now. She sobbed, "We need to cancel our party. It's in three weeks."

Henry turned to Ruthie and took her chin in his hand. Looking into her eyes, he said, "No, I don't want to cancel the party. The kids and grandkids have worked so hard on this. I can at least live three weeks. That's right, isn't it, Doc? I can make it twenty-one days?"

The specialist said, "I think so, Henry, but you never know."

Henry said, "That's all I need to hear. Thanks!"

The specialist gave him two prescriptions. Henry turned to Ruthie once more and, with tears running down his cheeks, said, "Ruthie, you have to *promise* me…*please* don't tell the kids, at least until after the party. Can you promise me that?"

Ruthie protested as best she could, but Henry insisted. At last, she agreed. They held hands as they walked out to their car.

Henry knew he had to get Ruthie one last gift. It had to be something specific, and he knew exactly who to call. He could only hope that his timing was right. (It was.) Henry rarely went anywhere without Ruthie these days, so when he told her he had to go by himself to run a little errand, she was very concerned. He said, "Don't worry, I won't be gone long," and he left. About two hours later, he returned.

Henry was in pain when he got home and limped inside. Ruthie ran to him as he sat down. He said, "I'm so sorry! I bought something for you, but I left it in the truck. Can you go out and get it?"

Ruthie took off his shoes and tilted his recliner back. She said, "I can get it later, whatever it is."

Henry kind of grinned a lopsided grin and said, "No, you'd better go now."

Ruthie asked, "What have you done, Henry?" She was on the verge of crying as she went out to his truck.

There, sitting on the passenger side, was a blond female golden-doodle puppy with a yellow bow around her neck. When she picked the puppy up, she was rewarded by getting her face licked multiple times. She was crying as she carried the puppy in to Henry.

Henry said, "I don't want you to be alone." He smiled at her.

She smiled back at Henry and said, "I love the yellow ribbon. I'm going to name her Daisy."

Over the next few days, Henry took his medicine as often as possible. He avoided doing things too strenuous because he knew he would cry out in pain. When the kids or grandkids came around, he was always sitting down at the kitchen table, the dining room table, or in his easy chair. Daisy was usually on his lap. Henry was pleased that no one seemed to notice his lack of energy.

The big day came. The kids had all split up the chores. All the girls would go to the beauty parlor with Ruthie to get their hair done and have manis and pedis. They had previously all helped Ruthie pick out and purchase a new special dress just for tonight. All the men had agreed to make sure Henry had on his tuxedo and would be there on time. Henry made sure they were all busy doing things and wouldn't notice him struggling into his tux.

Adam came and knocked on the door. As he opened it, he saw his father wince in pain. "Dad! What's wrong?" He rushed to the chair where Henry was.

Henry said, "It's okay, just a little indigestion." And he smiled.

Adam said, "Tell me the truth, Dad. That wasn't indigestion!"

Henry took a deep breath and said, "I guess you will have to know early. I'm going to need some extra help tonight." He took Adam's hands and told him everything.

Adam, now crying himself, said, "We need to call and cancel the party right now!"

Henry said, "No, son, we aren't going to cancel. The days ahead are going to be hard on your mother. I know you will all be here for her, but I want her to have this time with her family and friends. I want to celebrate loving your mother for fifty years. Even more importantly, I want to celebrate her loving me. Just help me tonight, please, and don't tell anyone."

Adam agreed. When they opened the door, Sebastian was standing there. He could see they both had been crying. He was immediately concerned. "What's wrong? What happened?"

Adam said, "Don't worry, buddy. They're just tears of happiness. Happy because my mother has loved this man so much since third grade!"

Henry added, "And I have loved her *so* much! I always have, I always will!" They went out to the cars.

When they got to the hotel, Adam helped his father get out. They walked to the banquet room with Adam's arm draped around his father's shoulders, as if they were best friends. In reality, he was steadying Henry and partially holding him up. He seated his father at his place of honor at the family table. As everyone had expected, the whole room was done with white twinkle lights. The colors of flowers on each table had been picked by G, and they were spectacular. Just then, Ruthie walked in with all her girls. Henry immediately choked up. She was so beautiful. Senator Champion, who had flown in just for this, simply said, "Wow!" as he shook Henry's hand.

Adam helped Henry up and said, "Let's go see Mom!" He walked him across the dance floor to Ruthie. When they got close, they could see Amanda had been crying. She looked at Adam and mouthed, "I know too."

No one had known the situation when they had picked the music for Henry and Ruthie's first dance. It was a favorite from their dating days, Elvis Presley singing "I Will Remember You." The words were now so very poignant. Ruthie started to cry.

Adam said, "Just go sit down, Mom and Dad. No one will think anything of it."

Henry pulled incredible strength and resolve from somewhere deep inside. He straightened his back, took Ruthie's hand, and said, "I would think something of it. Let me dance with your mother one more time." And he escorted Ruthie onto the dance floor. No one watching would have ever known anything was wrong with Henry's health as they danced.

Henry and Ruthie seemed to really enjoy spending the evening with their family and friends. It was a relief to not have to keep the secret from their family anymore. Adam and Amanda tried several times to get them to go home and rest, but they wouldn't leave.

When the guests had all left and the family was gathered around them, Henry put his arm around Ruthie and said, "You will never know how much this evening means to me and your mother. We couldn't have planned anything better. It has truly been a special evening. We came here to celebrate fifty years of marriage, but you—each of you—is really a celebration of our love. Your lives, what you have done with them, and what you will do with them are a testament to our love. People have asked me what I hope to pass on. I'm not completely sure how to answer that, but in seeing each of you, I know that I, *we*, have been successful. Thank you all *so* much. I can never express how very much I love each of you. Please remember that." He turned to look long at each of them, and they left.

They got home, heading up the road to the huge Christmas tree. The individual lights had blinked off due to their timer, but the big star at the top was still burning brightly. The grandkids all said hurried goodbyes and left so Henry and Ruthie could get to bed. Carrie and Dennis said their goodbyes and went to the cars to wait on their spouses.

Amanda started to cry hard now. Henry hugged her. She said, "Dad, oh, Dad…please don't leave us. I can't believe you aren't going to be here every day when I come! Please don't die, Daddy!"

Henry hugged her tighter and said, "You will be just fine. It will hurt for a while, but it will get better. Just know that when you come here, I *will* be here for you. I will be with you every day! Promise me that you and Adam will look after Mom." She nodded. He said, "Now go on and enjoy your life! I love you *so* much!" He gently pushed her out the front door.

Adam was standing with his arm around Ruthie. Henry could see that Adam was trying so hard to be strong. Adam said, "Don't worry, Dad, I promise you…" But that's all he could say before he started crying.

Henry went to them and said, "I know you will take care of your mother, Adam. I know you are strong and that *all* of you will be okay. I will be watching over each of you. Please know I have loved *you* so much! Now please go and enjoy your life. Remember that everything always works out if you try as hard as you can." He pushed Adam slowly out the door.

Henry and Ruthie watched the cars driving down the long driveway and turning out onto the main road by the Christmas tree. Ruthie turned to him and said, "Hurry up now, and let's get you to bed."

Henry asked, "Can we just sit out here on the porch swing for just a few minutes? I'd like to look at all those stars—there must be millions of them tonight—for just a few more minutes." He gave her his biggest smile, and she knew.

She helped him into the swing and sat down beside him. He said, "You know, you've always been beautiful. But tonight, you were the most beautiful of all." He kissed her hand as she started crying. "I am *so* sorry we don't have more time together." He put her hand on his chest, over his heart, and said, "I have loved you with all my heart for all my days. Can I rest my head on your shoulder? I'm so tired."

She said, "Yes, my love, rest your head."

After a few minutes, she felt his hand go limp in hers and knew he was gone. She sat there beside him for a little while, swinging very gently and crying. Then she gently laid him on the swing and went in to call Amanda and Adam.

Henry's funeral was everything you might have expected. Former President Forrester's son, daughter, and their families came. President Forrester and his wife had passed away previously, but the family still remembered the last trip on Air Force One, the wedding, and especially dropping the newlyweds off for their honeymoon. Senator Champion (Uncle Bruce), Aunt Patti, their four daughters (and two spouses), and six grandchildren all attended. Most of the town wanted to come. Cards also came in from all over the world. The service was held at the grave site, as no church in town could seat all the mourners. The service was just as Henry would have wanted it—simple and full of love and support. Although Aunt Patti wasn't sure she could do it, the family had asked her to sing "The Lord's Prayer." The funeral ended with this song, and Aunt Patti did a magnificent job!

Due to his popularity, Henry was allowed to be buried under his Christmas tree at the far end of the property. One day, Ruthie would rest there beside him.

Afterward, there was a brief reception. Nearly everyone got to speak to each of the family members. There were many tears, hugs, and loving words. Ruthie was so proud of her family as they stood with her. She was just as proud of Henry and all these people that had turned out to honor her husband. Henry had been a very special man. She had been blessed to spend most of her life with him.

Time slowly passed after the funeral. The days turned into weeks. Things for the family seemed to take a downturn. The Whitaker farm where Amanda had first begun to ride horses was put up for sale. This broke her and Alexandria's hearts. They had such history together there. The problem was the price. Although Amanda and Dennis would have loved to buy it, they couldn't afford the nearly $2,000,000 price tag.

Also, the two warmblood horses that Alexandria loved so much, Annabelle and Marie, were also offered for sale at $70,000 each. You could also purchase the custom trailer and truck that they were transported in for another $100,000. Alexandria cried when she heard this. It was as if she was losing two great friends! There was no way she could buy the horses, much less the truck and trailer.

Genevieve went to work at her job, only to find out the owner had received an offer to buy the business and had decided to sell. Genevieve was devastated. She said to the owner, "We have talked about this! I intended to work here until I could afford to buy you out."

The owner said she knew, but she didn't want to keep waiting. She wanted to enjoy life. G couldn't believe how this was turning out.

Meanwhile, at Adam's house, things seemed to be going the same way. Sebastian's star had been rising at the lab where he worked. Having been there, working in diversified areas for a few years, he was well-known. The owner had approached Sebastian and three of his associates that were just as smart and friends too. He offered to sell them the lab, but each of them had to come up with $200,000. The other three had wealthy fathers and could easily get the money. Sebastian knew there was no way he could come up with this money. The deal looked so great, but he couldn't make it happen.

And that left Adelyn. The little French bistro where she worked had brought in a new chef, John, for the entrees. He was a great guy, cute, very talented, and everyone thought the food he created was superb. He and Adelyn had begun dating, and it looked like it was going to get serious. They had talked about one day owning a place "just like this" and running it as husband and wife. They sketched pictures, drew up menus, even talked about what the wait staff would wear.

One day, they arrived at the bistro, and the owner was waiting for them. She told them she was very sorry but she had decided to sell the bistro. Her two grown sons had married and had to move away for their jobs. Her husband had died a few years previously, so she was all alone. She had decided she would move out to California where the rest of the family was. A side benefit was there was no snow...ever.

Adelyn was nearly in tears. She blurted out, "What if John and I bought it from you? Could you hold a mortgage for us? What kind of down payment would we need?"

The owner, Marguerite, said she would love for them to buy it. She also said she would be happy to hold the mortgage. The down payment would be 20 percent of the restaurant's selling price, not counting the equipment. The selling price would be based on the restaurant's annual revenues. Marguerite had the receipts and tax forms from the last five years showing the restaurant was averaging $20,000 per week. They would need a down payment of $210,000.

John looked at Adelyn. "How much can you come up with? I can probably borrow $50,000, but I have no money put away."

Adelyn shook her head, saying she had no money saved and probably not much credit. Another career, dream, or future seemed to be going up in smoke.

A week passed, but nothing changed for anyone. Ruthie asked everyone over for Sunday lunch, hoping to cheer them up. No one felt like going, but out of a sense of loss *and* love, everyone went.

Everyone gathered in the kitchen to enjoy each other's company. The aromas were all wonderful. Ruthie had bought a large rib roast as the centerpiece of the meal. She also served homemade yeast rolls, grilled asparagus, dirty rice, and a Caesar salad. Adelyn had been coaxed into making dessert. She had outdone herself with cherries jubilee. When everyone had finished and cleaned up the dishes, Ruthie asked them to join her back at the dining room table.

This was getting weird. Rib roast was always the family's go-to meal for Christmas and celebrations. There was nothing anyone could think of to celebrate. Now they were back at the table? They wrote it off to all the upheaval in the family's life and that Ruthie was just trying to lift their spirits.

When everyone was seated, except for her, Ruthie went into her bedroom and returned with four boxes and eight envelopes. She sat down and began, "I'm going to tell you a story and give out a few things. Some of this will be unbelievable to you. Maybe you will laugh, maybe you will cry, but it's very important to me that you hear me out and not interrupt. Does everyone agree?"

They all looked at one another with a little concern, but they all nodded and said yes.

You could see tears in her eyes as she continued, "First I have to tell you that this was completely Henry's idea, and I completely agreed. We had talked about it for a few months and then were planning on having you over for this dinner soon after our party. Your father and grandfather loved each of you so very much. I wish he was here to see your faces after I tell you the story.

"You all know that this family never did without. Henry made sure that we always had everything we needed. What he always had a surplus of was love. We never needed much money, so we saved all we could. I will get to that in just a few minutes.

"Back in 1980, we had been married almost ten years. We didn't have many bills or any children. I had been teaching almost ten years, and we had saved everything I made, knowing I would stop when we started having children. Uncle Bruce was hobnobbing back then with a lot of political figures that were in influential positions. He called late one evening, talked politely for a few minutes, and then got to the point. He asked Henry how much money we had in savings. Henry and Bruce were always best friends and loyal to a fault, so Henry told him. We had $50,000.

"Uncle Bruce told him to get up the next morning, withdraw *all* the money in a cashier's check, and take it to Bruce's local stockbroker, Terry Simpson. Bruce said there was a hot new stock that everyone in the upper echelons of politics was investing in. Bruce told Henry to invest our total nest egg, all $50,000 in this stock. He also told us to never withdraw anything—just let the dividends reinvest and buy more stock. Henry was okay with investing some, but not all of it. Bruce was emphatic. After he hung up, we talked about it. We knew I was going to be working a while longer, and we could at least rebuild part of our savings. Henry had always trusted Bruce. We agreed, and the next morning, Henry took our total nest egg to Terry and invested in the stock."

Ruthie stopped to take a sip of her sweet tea. No one said anything. This was a part of their history that no one had ever heard before. Ruthie continued, "Your father and grandfather and I had many talks about how best to help each of you. He didn't want you to have to wait until after we were gone to enjoy any money we had accumulated. He wanted to give it to you now and see you enjoy it. I know he must be in heaven, smiling right now, as I tell you this last part. The stock that Bruce told us to invest in was Walmart. Our $50,000 investment has turned into 372,000 shares of stock, currently valued at $19,500,000."

There was a crash as Adam fell out of his chair. Sebastian helped his father up, and Ruthie went on. "Henry and I worked so hard over the last months, talking to folks we knew and swearing everyone to secrecy. Let's start with the presents first. We usually go from oldest to youngest. Today, let's reverse that." She handed a beautifully wrapped box to Adelyn. She smiled and said, "Remember, Adelyn, this is what your granddaddy and I wanted you to have."

Adelyn opened the box and pulled out a fancy chef's hat. Everyone clapped as she put it on. "I love it!" she said.

Ruthie said, "There's more. Look in the bottom of the box."

Adelyn reached in and pulled out an envelope with legal documents and a small keychain with two keys on it. She looked at Ruthie inquiringly. Ruthie said, "Those are the keys to *your* French bistro. Granddaddy personally negotiated this deal with Marguerite. You will see his signature at the bottom of the contract. You have forty-eight hours to decide whether you want the restaurant. If not, the down payment will revert back to a trust we have set up for you."

Adelyn jumped up and ran to hug Ruthie, her chef's hat and all. She returned to her seat and, smiling, signed the contract for her French bistro. Everyone clapped.

"Okay, little G, you're up next." Ruthie handed G her present. She opened her box. Inside was an envelope and a key ring with several keys. Ruthie said, "Granddaddy and I have watched you blossom since you were first brought home. Your love of colors and fashion have only grown stronger through the years. We were so thrilled when you went to work in the field you love so much. We wanted you to have a job that you were passionate about, and you have that. When Granddaddy heard the owner was going to sell the store, he met with her privately and worked out another deal. In the envelope is the contract. You also have forty-eight hours to accept or decline. Three of the keys are to the store.

"The fourth key, a car key, was all Granddaddy's idea. He said you needed a pop of color in front of the store to draw even more attention to it. If you go out to the barn, Toby is waiting for you. He will let you inside where…"

Genevieve was crying. "Is it…is it?"

Ruthie said, "Yes, it's what you always wanted…it's a purple Lamborghini."

G shrieked and jumped up, knocking her chair over. She picked the chair up, ran to hug Ruthie, and ran shrieking out the front door. Everyone laughed as they watched her run across the long deep lawn in her dress and high heels.

"Your turn, Sebastian." Ruthie handed him his present. Sebastian's box contained two thick envelopes marked #1 and #2, a Chicago Cubs hat (which he immediately put on), and a key ring. "The key ring and envelope number 1 go together. Inside the envelope is your contract, giving you 25 percent ownership of Tri County Laboratory. You also have forty-eight hours."

Sebastian said, "I don't even have to think about this." And he signed his name.

Ruthie said, "The keys are to the building. Your other envelope was also completely Granddaddy's idea. He remembered taking your father to Wrigley Field to see the Cubs play. Then, years later, your father took you. He wanted you to be able to continue that tradition, either with your father or your own family one day. Inside the envelope are four season tickets to the Chicago Cubs games, field level, behind first base. Also, there is a small trust whose sole purpose is to invest dividends and buy those tickets, or upgrade them, for as long as you want."

Sebastian had no words. He and Adam both got up, moved around the table, and hugged Ruthie.

Finally, Ruthie turned to Alexandria and handed her present to her. Inside the box was a beautiful bridle and a key chain. "Your Granddaddy was especially excited when he was able to make this deal, Pumpkin Tart. He has had his eye on this gift for a few years but could not get the owner to part with what he wanted. The week he received his diagnosis, the owner called him to say he had changed his mind and would sell. We signed the papers the day before our party. Out there in the stalls at the back of the barn are the two warmblood horses you loved so much—Annabelle and Marie. They are yours. The key ring is for the truck and trailer that was designed for them. It's behind the barn."

Alexandria laid her head against Ruthie and cried, "Oh, Grandma! All of us have loved you and Granddaddy so very much over the years. And now this…my heart is so full of love and happiness. It's almost too much to bear."

Alexandria had wondered why G hadn't come racing back from the barn in her Lambo. Now she knew. G couldn't keep a secret to save her life. She must have decided to stay out there until Alexandria knew what her present was. Alexandria excused herself and walked to the door. She turned back at the door to smile at her family, and then she closed the door and ran to the barn to see her horses.

Ruthie turned back and said, "Okay, now for the adults. Once again, I remind you to please hear me out. Don't interrupt or say anything until I am through…please?"

Everyone nodded. Ruthie passed out eight envelopes, each one with a child or grandchild's name on it. She put Alexandria's and Genevieve's at their places.

Ruthie drew a deep breath. She was almost through. She continued, "Inside each of the adult's envelopes is a cashier's check. The taxes have already been taken care of. Inside each grandchild's envelope is a trust. The money in the trusts can only be spent by the child with parental consent until the child reaches thirty. At that time, it becomes completely theirs.

"The amount of each of your checks and each of the grandchildren's trusts is the same. Each check and trust is $2,000,000. Henry must be laughing and clapping his hands as he sees your faces right now! Amanda, what you want to do with your money is completely up to you, but might I suggest that you call the Whitakers and offer to buy the farm you've always loved before someone else does. Alexandria might need to keep her horses there for a while, but with the huge stables there, it shouldn't be a problem." Amanda ran to get her phone.

Adelyn married John, and their little bistro became a huge success. Over a short period, they opened five more locations, and all were successful. They had two little boys, Christian and David.

Sebastian and his partners built the lab into a huge success, inventing processes and patenting them over the years. He married one of Uncle Bruce's granddaughters, who had grown into a lovely young woman. They had three girls—Little Ruthie, Charlotte, and Rachel.

Genevieve had turned out to be the pickiest. Her perfect match had to not only be a great guy, but also *"must* have great fashion sense." She finally met a guy who truly did check all the boxes. She married Cullen, and they had two boys and two girls—Daniel, little Dennis, Kate, and Sarah.

Alexandria met her soul mate at a horse show. He was someone who loved horses just as much as she did. He was also handsome, polite, and very kind. Alexandria married David in the chapel in the trees in the fall. She rode in on the same sleigh that had carried her grandmother many years ago. The white twinkle lights had obviously been replaced, but they were all burning brightly for the wedding. They had two boys and a girl. They named them Henry, Bruce, and Vivian.

Ruthie turned ninety. She had become frail and needed help regularly. Amanda moved her into the mother-in-law suite she and Dennis had built on their farm for just that purpose. It was large, airy, and bright with walls painted a pale yellow. All the kids, grandkids, and great-grandkids visited her often. Everyone loved her so much, and she loved each of them just as much or more.

The time came when it was time to say goodbye. She was sleeping more and more. The doctor had visited and said he doubted she would make it through the night.

Amanda and Dennis moved her bed into the large den where the twenty plus loved ones could gather around her. She would open her eyes and smile as she looked around the room. There were quiet tears and hugs everywhere. Adam had his arm around Amanda and was whispering how lucky and blessed they were to have had the parents they did and, looking around the room, what a legacy Henry and Ruthie had produced.

Ruthie opened her eyes, and with sudden clarity, she looked from one to the next, locking eyes and blowing kisses to each one. She said, "I have loved you all so much from the very start. I always have and I always will." She closed her eyes one last time and was gone.

*****

Forever and Ever

When she opened her eyes, Ruthie immediately smiled a huge smile. There was Henry, young and handsome, dressed in his flannel shirt and khakis. He had a huge smile and was holding out his arms to her. She looked down and realized she was young again too. She was in her favorite blue dress. She ran to him and jumped into his arms. He hugged her tight and said, "I have missed you *so* much!" She knew that she was home.

About the Author

For the last ten years, David has been a high school reading teacher. His job was to bring the juniors and seniors who were assigned to him, usually reading two to four years beneath grade level, as close to grade levels as possible in order to pass state mandated tests. These were all students that had fallen behind, never caught up, and didn't like to read. If they couldn't pass the state tests, they were not able to receive their high school diplomas. David's personal three ways of helping them receive their diplomas were (1) starting out with lower level reading material and gradually increasing those levels, (2) offering them a wide range and length of materials, and (3) getting them to believe in themselves! He wanted them to be interested in finding out what happens next. He wanted to teach them to enjoy reading, and he was able to do that with help from his fellow teachers. Last year, 92 percent of David's students earned their diplomas! The reward of seeing these students, who had come so far, walk across the stage and get their diplomas is something David will always remember and cherish. His students inspired him to write this story about believing in yourself and being the best you can be, no matter what happens. I hope you enjoy the story of Henry, the little tree, and the family he loves so much!

CPSIA information can be obtained
at www.ICGtesting.com
Printed in the USA
JSHW020854101119
2352JS00003B/24

9 781645 841333